T R E

HORROR

STORIES

TRUE HORROR STORIES

Terry Deary

Hippo

Scholastic Children's Books,
Scholastic Publications Ltd,
7-9 Pratt Street, London NW1 OAE, UK

Scholastic Inc.,
730 Broadway, New York, NY 10003, USA

Scholastic Canada Ltd,
123 Newkirk Road, Richmond Hill,
Ontario, Canada L4C 3G5

Ashton Scholastic Pty Ltd,
PO Box 579, Gosford, New South Wales,
Australia

Ashton Scholastic Ltd,
Private Bag 1, Penrose, Auckland,
New Zealand

First published by Scholastic Publications Ltd, 1993

Copyright © Terry Deary, 1993

ISBN 0 590 55250 3

The right of Terry Deary to be identified as the author of this work has been
asserted by him in accordance with the Copyright, Designs and Patents Act, 1988.

Typeset by Contour Typesetters, Southall, London
Printed by Cox & Wyman Ltd, Reading, Berks.

10 9 8 7

Contents

For Debbie with thanks

INTRODUCTION

Newcastle, England – April 1992

The building I worked in used to be a huge private house. The downstairs rooms were large and grand with tall windows – but the higher you climbed the smaller and darker the corridors and rooms became.

My office was on the top floor. This must have been where the servants lived in the old days of the splendid hall.

One Thursday morning, at eleven o'clock, I reached the top landing and pulled open the door that led into a dimly-lit corridor. As I began to walk through the doorway a figure rushed towards me. It was a woman. She was small – the top of her head would have barely reached my chin. She had white hair, a long grey dress and a white apron.

I could see in that moment that her white-haired head was bent forward – she wasn't looking where she was going. There was no time or space for me to get out of her way. I flinched, closed my eyes and turned my head. I waited for the collision.

It never came. I opened my eyes. I blinked. There was no one there. I laughed at my own stupidity and forgot about the grey-haired, grey-dressed woman.

I returned to the building about seven-thirty that night. There was a late meeting in the great hall downstairs. My notes were in my office at the top of the stairs.

"Is the office open?" I asked the caretaker.

An old cleaner who'd worked in the building for over twenty years overheard me.

"You're not going upstairs at this time of night, are you?" she asked.

"Why not?" I shrugged.

"You wouldn't catch me going up there after dark . . . not for a million pounds."

"I'm not scared of the dark," I told her.

She shook her head. "Be careful . . . you might meet the Grey Lady!"

"Grey Lady?" I asked and felt a cold slug of fear run down my back. Somehow I knew what the cleaner was going to say.

"Yes! Didn't you know? The top floor's haunted by an old servant."

It was growing dark outside – and darker inside by now. This time my hand was trembling, just a little, as I reached the door at the top of the stairs. And I saw . . . nothing.

But what had I seen that morning? Perhaps I imagined I'd seen a woman in grey . . . but I'd never heard about the grey lady when I met her. Perhaps I'm a liar . . . only I can be certain that I'm not. Or perhaps I saw a ghost . . . a real horror from another world.

What is certain is that I wanted to know more about the supernatural. That's when the strangest thing of all happened. The day after I'd seen (or imagined) the Grey Lady, I received a letter. It asked me if I'd write a collection of true horror stories.

Here it is. A collection of ghosts and ghouls and murders and mysteries to make you wonder and to make you think.

Everyone loves a good chilling tale. But are there really such horrifying things in this world? Look at some of the stories here – stories that some people at some time have sworn are true. Then look at some of the facts that surround those stories and try to make up your mind.

Truth or lies? Fake or mistake?

But take care not to read them after dark! YOU HAVE BEEN WARNED!

LIZZIE B°RDEN'S
·A·X·E·

Some murders are so horrible that they are remembered long, long after.

Fall River, USA – 1892

The Bordens were the most important family in the town of Fall River. They had been there for hundreds of years. Yet the Bordens' house was not so very grand. Old Andrew Borden was too careful with his money for that. A cold, hard, loveless man, in 1892 he was seventy years old. He would not live to see seventy-one.

Number 92 Second Street was comfortable enough for Andrew Borden and his family. Comfortable but not grand. The house was warm in winter. Down in the basement was a coal-fired furnace. Near the furnace was a chopping block with a stack of wood for lighting the fire. And near the chopping block was an axe for splitting the wood into sticks.

There were four women in the house: Andrew's daughters Emma and Lizzie, their step-mother, Abby Borden, and the maidservant, Bridget. Mrs Abby Borden was sixty-three years old in 1892. She would not live to see sixty-four.

Abby never managed to take the place of Emma and Lizzie's mother in the hearts of the two young women. Number 92 Second Street was not a happy house.

Lizzie was thirty-two in 1892. She had learned meanness from her father. So she was disgusted and angry when her father gave a gift of land to his wife's family. She never forgave and she never forgot – something seemed to snap in Lizzie's strange mind.

"Lizzie!" Mrs Abby Borden said one day. "I haven't seen my cat for ages. Do you know where he is?"

Lizzie wasn't beautiful, but her large, light eyes were the most attractive thing about her. "Go downstairs and you'll find your cat," she promised, and those eyes glowed with pleasure.

Mrs Borden went down to the cellar and found the cat . . . it had been laid across the chopping block and someone had cut off its head with the wood axe.

But that was nothing to what happened on the morning of 4 August 1892. A hot and humid morning. Even at a quarter past six in the morning, the sun was blazing hot as maidservant Bridget struggled downstairs to light the cooking stove. She felt ill. Everyone in the house had been ill the day before – maybe from eating meat that had gone bad in the summer heat. Emma was spared because she was away on holiday.

After breakfast Mrs Borden went upstairs to lie down. She was still unwell from the food-poisoning of the day before. Mr Borden went into town to do business while Bridget set about cleaning the windows.

By twenty to eleven Mr Borden had returned. He struggled with the locks on the front door. Someone had pushed the bolt in so hard that Bridget could hardly open it to let her master in.

Lizzie stood at the top of the stairs. She laughed.

Mr Borden strode in. "Where's your mother?"

"Out. She had a message to go and visit someone who's sick," Lizzie answered.

"Who?"

"I don't know, Father."

"They can't be sick as me," the old man snapped. "I still feel weak from yesterday. I think I'll lie down in the sitting room."

Lizzie smiled. It was two minutes to eleven. Bridget went back to washing windows as Lizzie set up an ironing board and started ironing handkerchiefs.

"Excuse me, Miss Lizzie, but I feel sick again," the girl groaned. "If you don't mind I'll just lie down." The maidservant climbed up to her attic bedroom. The City Hall clock was striking eleven.

Bridget lay down on her bed. Ten minutes later she heard

Lizzie cry out, "Bridget! Oh, Bridget! Come down!"

Bridget struggled from her bed. "What's wrong, Miss Lizzie?"

"Come down quickly! Father's dead! Somebody's come in and killed him!" Lizzie shouted.

Bridget went to the sitting room to look. Lizzie stopped her. "No! Don't go in there. Go and get a doctor! Run!"

But Bridget couldn't find the local doctor. She left a message with the doctor's wife and hurried back to number 92 Second Street.

"How did it happen?" the girl groaned. "Where were you, Miss Lizzie?"

"In the garden," Lizzie Borden sighed. "When I came back in the door was open wide."

A neighbour, Mrs Churchill, saw the frantic women and came across to find out what was wrong. She opened the door to the sitting room. Andrew Borden lay on the settee where he'd gone to rest. His feet were on the floor. His head was resting on the arm. But it was a head that no one would have recognised.

There were eleven cuts between his nose and ear; one blow had sliced his eye in half and another had almost cut his nose clean off. Blood spattered the floor, the wall, the sofa – but Andrew Borden hadn't moved. His murderer had slaughtered him as he slept.

Mrs Churchill backed out of the room. "Where were you when it happened?" she gasped.

"In the barn," Lizzie murmured.

"Your poor mother must be told. Where is she?"

Lizzie shrugged, helpless. "She went to visit a sick friend. I don't know who."

Mrs Churchill took charge. She sent messages for the doctor and the police. By half past eleven she had returned to the house of death on Second Street.

"If only we could find your mother, Lizzie. Maybe we should send a message to her friend, Mrs Whitehead!"

"No!" Lizzie answered sharply. "I'm sure I heard her come in the front and go up to her room! Bridget, go and see."

But shaking, sickly Bridget wouldn't go alone.

"I'll go with you," Mrs Churchill offered. The two set off up the front stairs. They didn't need to climb quite to the top. The bedroom door was open. Bridget stopped. Behind the bed, half hidden, lay Abby Borden's body.

Mrs Churchill pushed past the rigid maidservant and looked at the gruesome sight. Nineteen blows had rained down on the back of her head and one had chopped deep into her neck. But the blood had dried and started to turn dark. It seemed that Abby Borden had died some time before her husband.

No note was ever found. The truth was that Abby Borden had never left the house. She must have died soon after breakfast.

And Lizzie had never gone into the barn. The floor was dry and thick with dust. The first policeman in the barn would swear that there was not a single footprint in the dust. Could Lizzie have lied?

Lizzie was the one the police suspected. But Lizzie was a Borden. A lady from the finest family in Fall River. Surely she could not have butchered both her stepmother and her father . . . could she?

In that hot house which was home to such cold, cold people, Lizzie Borden stayed cooler than ice. As her parents' corpses still lay in their blood-stained rooms she said calmly, "I think I'd prefer them to be buried by undertaker Winwood."

The next night, Lizzie placed an advert in the local paper:

$5,000 Dollar reward

The above reward will be paid to anyone who may secure
THE ARREST AND CONVICTION
of the person or persons who are responsible for the deaths of
MR ANDREW I BORDEN AND HIS WIFE

That same Friday the Fall River police found a new, amazing fact. The day before the murders Lizzie Borden had been to a local chemist's shop and tried to buy some prussic acid . . . perhaps the deadliest poison known!

On Saturday the funeral was held for Abby and Andrew Borden.

On Sunday Lizzie was seen trying to burn an old dress. "Why are you doing that?" a friend asked.

"It's covered with paint," she said.

"But it looks so suspicious, trying to burn old clothes! The police will say you're trying to hide blood stains!"

"Ah!" Lizzie gasped. "I didn't think. I only wish you'd stopped me!" But mean Lizzie Borden had burned a dress that was only ten weeks old . . . something unheard of in the penny-pinching Borden house.

And one week after the murders the Fall River police arrested Lizzie Borden for the crime. The trial was almost a year later and in the middle of another heat wave. It was ninety-three degrees Fahrenheit outside the courtroom and hotter still inside.

On a table lay a bag. It was covered with tissue paper. The lawyer threw a piece of evidence onto the table – one of Lizzie's dresses. The dress caught the bag and the tissue flew off. Now Lizzie could see what was in the bag – the shattered skulls of her father and stepmother! Lizzie fell into a dead faint at the shock. But the shock was not great enough to make her confess.

She sat silent through the days of the trial. At last her lawyer pleaded that the jury must either set poor Lizzie free, or be blamed for placing a hangman's noose around her neck. He reminded them that Andrew Borden had gone to his grave wearing a ring that was a gift from Lizzie. "To find her guilty," he finished, "you must find her a fiend! Does she look it?"

The twelve men of the jury looked at Andrew Borden's little

girl. Her large, pale eyes looked back. Eyes that had never shed a tear for the deaths. Yet, as her lawyer claimed,

> *"The eyes that cannot weep*
> *Are the saddest eyes of all."*

The judge turned to her and asked, "Lizzie Borden, have you any words you wish to say to this jury?"

She rose slowly to her feet, bowed to the judge and looked straight at the twelve men. "I am innocent. I leave it to my counsel to speak for me." Thirteen words. The only words that Lizzie Borden spoke at her own trial.

The jury voted. The clerk of the court asked, "Gentlemen of the jury, have you reached your verdict?"

"We have."

"What do you say?"

"Not guilty!"

A huge cheer swept the courtroom. Lizzie sat back in her seat and at last managed a tear – in sheer relief that her neck had been saved. "Take me home," she muttered. "Take me home. I want to go to the old place tonight."

And Lizzie went back to the house of death and lived with the ghosts of her butchered father and stepmother. She died thirty-four years after the trial, in 1927. Her sister, Emma, died nine days later.

Lizzie Borden left over a million dollars in her will. Some say that Lizzie got away with murder.

So who killed the Bordens?

There are three explanations. Read them all then decide which you think is the most likely.

The Hidden Killer – FACT FILE

1.   Mr Andrew Borden was not a popular man. There must have been many men and women in Fall River who wanted to see him dead.

2.   The killer slipped poison into the Bordens' milk on Wednesday morning, 3 August, 1892. It made them all sick but didn't kill them. So, on the morning of 4 August, the killer crept into the Borden house while Mrs Borden and Lizzie were upstairs. The maid, Bridget, rushed out to be sick and left the back door open. The killer waited.

3.   Mrs Borden received a note asking her to visit a sick friend. Mr Borden returned home feeling ill and lay down to sleep. The killer crept out and, with one of the axes from the Borden cellar, hacked Andrew Borden to death. The killer was forced to hide because Lizzie came back from the barn and started ironing in the next room.

4.   Lizzie discovered the body and Mrs Churchill sent for the police. While Mrs Churchill went for help, Mrs Abby Borden came home. The killer followed her upstairs and murdered her with the same axe. The killer escaped out of the front door while the police were coming to the back door.

This was Lizzie's explanation and the one the judge chose to believe – the trouble is the experts said that Mrs Borden died before Mr Borden, a fact the judge ignored. The public believed it at first; they spent days in terror believing a mad axe-man was on the loose in Fall River.

The Deadly Daughter – FACT FILE

1.   Lizzie hated her father and her stepmother. She waited till her sister had gone on holiday. Then, on Tuesday 2 August, tried to buy poison to get rid of them. The chemist wouldn't sell her poison but she found some somewhere. She slipped it into their food on Wednesday 3 August – she even gave herself a little so no one would suspect. It wasn't enough to kill them.

2.   On the morning of 4 August, when her father had left the house, she took an axe from the cellar, crept upstairs and hacked her stepmother to death. She had over an hour to clean herself up before her father came home.

3.   When her father came home and lay down to sleep she killed him too. She still had ten minutes to hide the axe and wash off the blood before she called Bridget down and told her that her father was dead. When Bridget asked where Mrs Borden was Lizzie panicked and came up with the stupid story that there had been a note calling her to a sick friend. Later, Lizzie was stuck with this story even after it was shown that her mother had been dead for over an hour and a half before this imaginary letter was delivered.

4.   When Mrs Churchill announced that she would have to search for Mrs Borden, Lizzie quickly invented the story that she'd heard her stepmother come into the house. She realised that all of the blood had not been washed out of her dress after the first killing, so she burned it. She gambled that a jury would not want to see a woman hang. She won her gamble.

This is the story believed by most people.

The Murderous Maid – FACT FILE

1.   Bridget had had enough of the Bordens. They were mean and thoughtless people to work for. She tried to poison them. She even took a little poison herself so that no one would suspect her. After all, Bridget did the cooking. She was the obvious person to put poison in the food.

2.   It didn't work on the Bordens but Bridget woke up feeling ill. Then, to cap it all, on one of the hottest days in the history of Fall River, Mrs Borden ordered Bridget to clean all of the windows, inside and out.

3.   Bridget sweated, carrying buckets of water from the barn and using a heavy brush to reach the upstairs windows. She went into the house to clean the inside windows and saw Mrs Borden kneeling on the floor over a large piece of embroidery. It was so easy!

4.   Bridget tiptoed downstairs, took the axe from the cellar and crept back to Mrs Borden's room. The old woman was still kneeling over the tapestry. Bridget raised the axe and smashed it down into the skull of the old woman. In a frenzy she kept smashing down until she was exhausted.

5. She took the chance to clean her dress the next time she went to the barn for water. When Mr Borden returned she made an excuse to Lizzie and said that she needed a rest. As Lizzie went out to the barn Bridget killed the sleeping Mr Borden. He was killed with fewer, weaker blows – Bridget was too exhausted to do more.

6. Lizzie came in and found the body. Bridget told Lizzie that Lizzie would be blamed! She suggested that a story about Mrs Borden called out of the house would help! And no wonder Bridget refused to go up to Mrs Borden's bedroom alone . . . she knew what she'd find!

This was the story put forward by one writer who studied the case.

There is a murder committed in the USA about once every half an hour. But the horrific Borden killings are still remembered whenever people meet together and the subject turns to murder. American children have no doubt who was to blame. They have a playground rhyme that goes:

> *Lizzie Borden took an axe*
> *And gave her mother forty whacks:*
> *When she saw what she had done*
> *She gave her father forty-one!*

NIGHTMARe F·A·R·M

*Some ghosts seem to haunt the place they died and act out the way they died
. . . to the horror of the living.*

Brittany, France – August 1951

It never rains but it pours, John Allen thought. He trudged
along the muddy French lane and cursed his luck.

He'd arrived in France that morning and stepped off the ferry
to enjoy his cycling holiday. First came the rain to spoil it. Then
cars rushing past him on the west roads had thrown up clouds of
drenching spray.

So John had turned off the main road and onto the quiet
country tracks, hoping for an easier journey. That was his first
mistake. The rain had grown heavier, but now he was in the
middle of the countryside with nowhere to shelter.

As he churned through muddy puddles, he didn't see the
broken bottle lying at the bottom of one of them. He heard the
splintering of the glass and the sudden bang as his tyre burst.

John sighed and climbed off his cycle to look at the damage. A
ripped inner tube. He carried a puncture repair kit, but this was
no small puncture – it was a large split. He tried to mend it. But
the rain washed over the rubber and no patch would stick. It
needed a new inner tube. He set off to push to the nearest
village. There'd been one five miles back. Surely the next one
must be closer. He went forward. That was his second mistake.

Two hours later and John had still not seen a living human or
a house. His feet and legs were thick with mud and the cycle
seemed five times heavier than when he'd set out.

He looked up, brushed the rain out of his eyes and saw a lone
house. Shelter and warmth, he thought. Not a village with a
bicycle repair shop, but a resting place at least. He turned off
the muddy lane and headed towards it. That was John's third,
and greatest, mistake.

The driveway was overgrown. The late afternoon was dull and dreary, but there were no lights in the windows. The house was large with fine, tall chimneys, yet there was no smoke coming from them. It had clearly been a farmhouse – there were barns and sheds at the side. And it had been a rich farmer's house, for behind it John could see that the gardens had their own lake.

His heart sank. It was obviously deserted now. No warm welcome here. At least, he thought, there'd be shelter. He could dry out and wait for the rain to stop.

He knocked at the heavy front door. The knock boomed through the empty house. He tried the door handle. To his surprise it was unlocked. John stepped into the gloom of the hall and wheeled his cycle in.

"Hello?" he called. There was no reply.

He propped his cycle against the wall and went into the living room. For some reason it was still furnished. The smell of damp and decay was powerful. But the fireplace looked inviting. John ran back through the rain to the barn where he found some scraps of dry wood and straw to make a blaze.

When he returned to the living room he almost dropped his armful of wood in fear. For there, in the dust of the floor, was a trail. It led from the locked french-windows across to the settee. Even in the shadowy room the trail glistened clearly. It was thick, wet slime.

John edged his way around it and placed the wood in the fireplace. His hands trembled as he tried to light a match. At last the fire flared into life. He could see that the trail ended at a sofa. In the flickering light he could now see something lying on the sofa.

He licked the rain off his chin, for his mouth had gone strangely dry. He peered at the rags on the sofa. They were the remains of a pair of pyjamas – muddy and mouldering and stinking. Worse, they made John suddenly afraid. He backed away.

A sudden draught blew out the fire and plunged the room back into its late-afternoon gloom. A sound in the hallway made him grab for a poker. The sound was of something wet and soft falling to the floor.

"Who's there?" John crept to the door and flung it open. Only his dripping cycle stood where he had left it.

He laughed at his own fears, then hurried back to light the fire again. "I'll be all right once I'm warm and dry," he muttered. "But I don't think I'll be staying the night."

Then that weird and chilling sound came from the doorway again. It seemed nearer now! A thick trail of slime was in the passageway. But worse . . . it was moving towards the room!

John backed away. The slime-trail followed him. His back was to the fireplace now but the trail didn't seem to be interested in him . . . yet.

It turned towards the sofa and the ragged pyjamas. As it reached the sofa the pyjamas seemed to jerk into life. First they rose up, lifted by an invisible hand. Then they began to swell out as if they were being filled by a living body. But it was an invisible body and a very wet one, for the pyjamas began to dribble with water.

John didn't wait to see what the pyjamas planned to do next. He ran. He ran through the doorway and through the hall, leaving the cycle behind. He rushed into the streaming rain without noticing it. He stumbled back down the tangled drive and onto the muddy lane.

His head down, he ran blindly into the fading evening shadows. He ran a mile before he came to the village. The local inn was the first building he came to. He burst through the door and stood, wild-eyed and weak-kneed at the bar.

The landlord looked at the Englishman with pity. He guided

him to a seat and pushed a large glass of brandy into his hand. John gulped at it thankfully. Everyone in the bar room was staring at him. In the warmth and light of the inn John suddenly felt his fears had been foolish. "Sorry," he said. "No money! It's with my cycle . . . in a house . . . down the road."

The landlord patted his shoulder. "Oui, monsieur. Tonight, stay here."

"My cycle . . ."

"We will fetch it tomorrow. Tonight you must rest."

"But that house!"

"We know all about the house, monsieur," the landlord said. "But tonight you rest."

In the warm bedroom of the inn, John slept – an exhausted sleep. It was the next morning when he began to unravel the terrible truth behind the farm. John spoke little French and the landlord just a little more English. With the help of three-year-old newspaper cuttings, they pieced together the story.

Just six years before, during the Second World War, the farm had been owned by a strange and lonely man, an artist called Marc Baus. Of course, the German army controlled the country at that time; the French were forced to work for them and obey them. Many brave French people resisted the mighty German army and tried to fight them. Many died in the attempt. Too many. Someone was betraying the French Resistance fighters to the Germans! Everyone in the village suspected Marc Baus.

When the war ended, Baus was brought to trial for his treachery. To the disgust of the villagers he was given just two years in prison. By 1948 he was back at his farm. They remembered the dead and their hatred of Baus boiled up. They marched to the farm and threatened to kill him. Their stones shattered his windows. Only the arrival of the local police saved his life.

But Baus was a frightened and friendless man. He was never seen again . . . alive. Two months after the stoning, his body was found in the little lake behind the house. The police took the dripping body into the house to examine it. The water and slimy weeds trailed across the floor of the living room as they carried it in. They laid the corpse on the sofa. Baus had been wearing pyjamas when he died.

The surgeon announced that he had drowned . . . he was not able to say how. Perhaps it was an accident. Perhaps it was suicide . . . perhaps it was murder of the most hated man in the region. The body was buried in a flowerless grave.

"You were not surprised when I came in last night," John Allen said.

The landlord shook his head. "You are not the first to shelter from a storm in that old house. Two years ago, two workers sheltered there . . . they saw the same as you, monsieur. Now no one ever goes into that house. Some braver men will bring your cycle . . . not me! I would not go near there again. No, not for twenty million francs!"

John nodded. "Nor would I," he shuddered. "Nor would I!"

The haunted farmhouse was demolished to make way for a new motorway. The ghost has not been seen since then.

Ghostly Evidence — FACT FILE

Many ghosts, like the one in the haunted French farmhouse, are said to leave some evidence of their presence other than their appearance . . .

1. **Water** Ghosts that have met watery deaths are said to leave wet footprints or perhaps a trail of slime when they return.

2. **Scent** In Bramshill House at Hartney Wintney in Hampshire, England, a bride with her wedding bouquet played hide-and-seek with her guests after the ceremony. But she became trapped in a chest and suffocated. The scent of her bouquet of lilies still hangs in the air when she appears. Her death is said to have happened in 1725. The house is now a police training establishment.

3. **Sounds** Ghosts are often heard if not seen. People living at the edge of battlefields have claimed to hear the sounds of clashing weapons and screams of the dead for centuries after.

4. **Touch** People who claim to have seen ghosts very often mention a freezing chill that comes with the ghost.

5. One of the most curious watery graves can be found in Massachusetts . . .

Underneath this stone
Lies poor John Round.
Lost at sea
And never found.

(Think about it!)

6.   It's reckoned that one person in ten will see a ghost in their lifetime . . . but not everyone will recognize it at the time. There are countless stories of people thinking they'd seen a friend (or relation), then finding out much later that the friend had already died.

7.   Children under ten years are more likely to see ghosts than people of any other age. Perhaps as people grow older they are afraid of being laughed at if they claim to have seen one. Or maybe adults try to explain away what they've seen, whereas children just accept it.

THE BODYSNATCHERS

Some people will do anything to make money. Two hundred years ago they did the most disgusting thing of all . . . they sold dead bodies.

Edinburgh, Scotland – 1827

"Good morning, Mr Desmond. Time to get up!" William Hare was the manager of the old boarding house. He kicked at the old man. Old Desmond didn't move. The only things moving on the filthy, straw-filled mattress were the fleas.

"Come along, Mr Desmond! All the others are out and about, on the streets begging!" Hare giggled. He had never been able to control that giggle. He rubbed his rough hands and looked proudly round the room. It was a good room. Only two metres by three but he'd packed three beds into it. With three men and women to each bed he could make a nice, fat profit from renting the sleeping places.

But he'd never make a profit from the likes of Old Desmond. The man was getting too feeble to beg. He hadn't paid for weeks. William Hare's eyes narrowed. "We don't want to have to put you out on the streets, now do we, Mr Desmond?" he said. The old man didn't reply.

"You owe three pounds already," Hare went on and kicked the man harder. He bent down and shook the pauper. "So get out there and earn it!"

But the old man was stiff and cold.

Hare gave a cry of rage. "Dead! Dead and owes me three pounds!"

The door swung open and a shorter, dark-haired man looked in. "Something wrong, Mr Hare?" William Burke asked. He had a small hammer in his hand and a scrap of leather. He took old shoes, patched them and sold them on the streets. Hare had rented out a tiny room at the back of the house for him to work in.

"Wrong? Aye, there's something wrong. Old Desmond here has died!" Hare snarled.

"May God have mercy on him," Burke murmured.

Hare gave a sudden, wild giggle. "May God have mercy on me!" he screeched. "The man owed me more than three pounds . . . nearly four!"

"That's sad, Mr Hare," Burke agreed. "If you like I'll call on the parish clerk to arrange to have him buried."

William Burke and William Hare got drunk. They sat on the floor of Burke's little cobbler workshop and stared at the rough, wooden coffin.

"Tell me again," Hare said softly. "How can I get my money out of the old man?"

"Sell his body," Burke answered carefully.

"Sell his body," Hare nodded and giggled. "You want to buy it, Burke?"

"No use to me. But they do say that the doctors in the town want bodies . . . and they are willing to pay."

"Four pounds?"

"Four pounds – two for you and two for me," Burke said.

"Can we do that?" Hare asked.

"No," his lodger said. "We can't do it legally. We have to do it secretly."

"But they'll come to bury him tomorrow!" Hare argued.

"We fill his coffin with some of the rubbish from this workshop. No one will ever know."

Hare nodded. "Pass me your hammer, Burke." He took it and began to work at the nails on the lid.

Doctor Knox looked at Burke and Hare with some disgust. "The body is not in perfect condition," he said. "I can only offer you seven pounds!"

Burke's jaw fell in surprise. Hare gave a sudden, wild giggle. "Seven pounds!"

The Doctor misunderstood. He thought the offer was too small. "Very well . . . seven pounds and ten shillings. Not a penny more!"

"We'll take it, sir!" Burke said quickly.

"But take the shirt away," Doctor Knox said angrily.

"The shirt?" Burke gaped. "We don't want it, sir."

"You stupid man!" the doctor exploded. "The body belongs to no living person. It is a crime for you to sell it, but it is not a crime for me to buy it. The shirt is different. The shirt belonged to the old man. I would go to prison if I was caught buying the shirt."

Hare shook his head, confused.

"If you bring me more bodies, bring them without clothes," the Doctor said.

"More?" Burke said sharply. "You want more?"

"We always need more," Doctor Knox said sadly.

"Why . . . sir?" Hare asked with a simpering grin.

"We are a medical school," the doctor explained. "How can we cure the sick if we don't understand how the body works? You wouldn't want us to cut you up while you were alive, would you?" Hare shuddered, shook his head and giggled nervously.

Doctor Knox sighed. "The law will only allow us to use the bodies of dead criminals. There are so precious few of those. Some fellows have taken to digging up bodies from graveyards," he said in a low voice. "Understand, I do not wish to know where you obtain your bodies. Just bring them to me." Suddenly he pointed a thin finger at the men. "You are doing a service to the world of medicine."

"Thank you, sir," Burke smiled.

"Thank you, sir," Hare cringed as they backed towards the door.

The two men slid out into the lampless Edinburgh night.

Burke and Hare were moody and restless. "Seven pounds and ten shillings, spent and gone," Burke groaned.

"Spent and gone," Hare giggled.

"It's a pity old Desmond isn't still with us," Burke sighed.

"Aye, then he could get sick and die again," Hare agreed. The two men sat silent for a while.

"Old Joseph's sick," Burke said softly.

"Sick but not dead," Hare reminded him.

"Aye, not dead . . . yet," Burke said. The silence fell between them like dust settling on the dirty table.

"He'll be dead soon," Burke went on.

"Not soon enough for me," Hare added viciously.

"And not soon enough for Joseph," Burke added gently. "It cannot be pleasant for the poor old soul to suffer like that."

Hare's little eyes glittered as he began to catch his partner's meaning. "Death would be a kindness," he said carefully.

Burke met Hare's eyes. "A kindness. And Joseph's friends would want to be kind to him – help him to die."

"Let him starve," Hare suggested.

"Too slow."

"Poison him?"

"Too painful."

"Wait till he falls asleep . . ."

"And smother him!"

"Pass me that pillow, Burke."

Doctor Knox gave the two men ten pounds for old Joseph's body. He asked no questions and didn't seem to notice how the old man had died. Doctor Knox found they were becoming reliable bodysnatchers. But they weren't bodysnatchers. They were murderers.

They weren't *taking* dead bodies . . . they were *making* dead bodies.

The poor people of Edinburgh kept disappearing, month after month – fourteen . . . fifteen . . . sixteen . . .

Burke and Hare began to lure the weak and the drunken to their lodging house. Sometimes they had unlikely allies in their work. One night, Constable Andrew Williamson found a drunken old woman asleep in the gutter. "Come along, lady, it's off to the jail with you. We'll give you a wooden bed and a cup of cold porridge."

He heaved her to her feet and began to struggle down the street with her. A watching figure slid from the shadows.

"Good evening, Constable Williamson," William Burke said softly.

"Ah!" the young policeman grunted. "Evening, Mr Burke."

"Who have we here?" the bodysnatcher breathed.

"Some old biddy who's got drunk on too much gin."

"Taking her home, are you?" Burke asked.

"To jail," Constable Williamson groaned as he struggled to hold the woman upright.

"Oh, but her family will worry," Burke frowned. "It would be a kindness if you'd let me take her home. I happen to know where she lives."

The young constable brightened. "Why, Mr Burke! It *is* a kindness, that's for sure," he said and passed the mumbling woman to the bodysnatcher.

"Goodnight, Mr Burke," the policeman smiled. "And thank you!"

"No!" Burke chuckled. "Thank *you!*" And he led another victim back to the boarding house.

As she snored on the louse-ridden bed, Burke lay on top of her to pin her arms and legs down. Then Hare placed a huge hand across her mouth and pinched her nose. The old woman struggled under Burke's great weight. She fought for breath. She tried to scream.

After a minute, the struggles grew weaker. A minute later they stopped . . . forever. Like many others she died of suffocation. Before the sun came up next morning, her frail old body was lying in a box in the surgeon's house.

Not all their victims died so easily. One old woman had her deaf-mute grandson with her. They killed the woman and planned to set the poor boy free – after all, he couldn't speak to tell his tale. But the boy was fretting and making a fuss. Burke was worried that somehow he might lead the police back to the boarding house.

He took the boy into the back room and broke his spine across his knee. The bodies were packed in a pickled-herring barrel and taken off to Surgeon's Square.

But Burke and Hare grew greedy. Burke and Hare grew careless. The police received a terrible report. A couple called Grey had stayed in the boarding house and met an old lady called Docherty. The next morning the old lady had vanished. As Mrs Grey cleaned up the bedroom the next day, she saw blood on the straw of the bedding. And under the straw lay a lifeless arm . . . it belonged to the dead Mrs Docherty.

The Greys left the body and Mr Grey went to the police. Constable Fisher investigated. "When did you last see Mrs Docherty?"

"Last night at seven," Burke lied. "She left the house last night and no one's seen her since."

The constable thought that Burke was an honest man. He believed him at first and went in search of Burke's wife. "When did you last see Mrs Docherty?" he asked her.

"Oh, at seven o'clock this morning," she told him. "She spent the night at our house."

Constable Fisher was puzzled. Someone was lying. The old woman's body was found at Knox's surgery. The police doctor examined it. He reported that Mrs Docherty could have been suffocated – but, then again, she could have died of natural causes.

The police were sure that Burke and Hare were guilty of murder. But one dead old woman and a few lies don't make a murder case. What they needed was someone who had seen a murder. A witness.

And a witness did come forward. He had seen Burke commit more than one killing. Who was this witness? Burke's old partner, William Hare! For the frightened Hare had made a deal – the police said that he could go free, but only if he went to court and put the blame on Burke. The cowardly Hare agreed.

On 28 January 1829 William Burke went to the gallows. He was sorry for his crime – but still angry that Knox hadn't paid him in full for that last dead body. The money could have bought him a fine coat for his execution!

The crowd gathered to watch Burke die. They howled their hatred at the man who, they said, had killed thirty harmless people. The rope was short and Burke did not die instantly. As the crowds cheered he died slowly and in agony, gasping for breath . . . just as so many of his victims had done.

And, when he was dead, his body was handed over to the doctors to be cut up for their experiments.

The nineteenth-century streets of Edinburgh were just a little safer.

Bodysnatching – FACT FILE

1. Bodysnatchers usually dug up bodies after they had been buried. Someone who rises from the dead is said to be resurrected. Because they "raised the dead", bodysnatchers were often known as "Resurrectionists".

2. Families tried to protect their dead relatives' coffins by burying them under steel cages so they couldn't be dug up.

3. Some cemeteries had watch-houses built and put guards in with guns. Guards were often nervous, all alone in a graveyard at night. They would often shoot anything that moved. That probably explains how some cemetery guards in Aberdeen once killed a pig.

4. Bodysnatchers could make extra money by selling teeth from bodies to dentists. These teeth would then be used to make false teeth.

5. Bodysnatchers often worked in gangs. They kept some secrecy by using nick-names such as "Lousy Jack", "Praying Howard", "The Spoon" (because of his curious shovel), "The Mole" (because he was such a good digger), "The Screw" and "Merry Andrew".

6. "The Spoon" and "The Mole" were angry with "Merry Andrew" because they felt he'd cheated them of their share of bodysnatching money. When "Merry

Andrew's" sister died they decided to steal and sell her body. "Merry Andrew" guessed their game and let them dig her up. As soon as they had, he leapt out from behind a gravestone with a white sheet over him. They ran away. "Merry Andrew" took his own sister straight to the surgeons and sold her.

7. Two medical students, Henry and George, fell in love with the same girl. She preferred Henry and was heartbroken when he died. She wept over his grave. George was so jealous that he had Henry's body removed and sold. He then enjoyed watching the girl weeping and praying at the graveside. Only *he* knew it was empty soil!

8. Expert bodysnatchers used wooden spades because they were quieter than metal ones.

9. Bodysnatchers were also known as "Sack-'em-up men" because of the way they would dig 'em up, then sack 'em up.

10. Selling bodies to doctors stopped soon after Burke and Hare were caught. The law changed to allow surgeons to have more bodies legally.

DIARY OF A HORROR HOUSE

It's America's favourite true horror story with a best-selling book and a popular film based on it.

Amityville, New York, USA – 1965 to 1976

The house at 112 Ocean Avenue is a fine one. It stands on the edge of the Amityville River. It has its own boathouse, heated swimming pool, two-car garage, large living rooms and six bedrooms. It also has a tragic history.

1965 – Ronald DeFeo and his family move into 112 Ocean Avenue, Amityville. Ronald likes the place and puts up a name-board at the end of the garden saying, "High Hopes". The DeFeos are a religious family and there is a model of a religious scene on that lawn. They seem a normal and happy family.

November 1974 – Mr and Mrs DeFeo are still living at 112 Ocean Avenue with their five children. They would be happy if it weren't for the oldest son, Ronnie. Ronnie is spoilt. He has been in trouble with the police on more than one occasion. Ronnie has been charged with theft – even though he has all the money he needs – and with taking drugs. Early this month he is suspected of being mixed up in a $19,000 robbery. This is the last straw. His father throws him out of the house.

13 November 1974 – Ronnie runs into a local bar and cries, "My father and mother have been shot!"

The men from the bar rush to 112 Ocean Avenue and find the whole family in their beds. Each one has been turned face down on their bed and shot with a high-powered rifle. The killer has rested their heads on their arms. The men from the bar call the police.

The police discover that the victims had all been drugged at supper that night. The killer must have done this so he could return and kill them without disturbing anyone. The killer must have been someone very close to the family.

The murder weapon is found. Ronnie is arrested. He is accused of drugging his family so they fell deeply asleep. As they slept, he shot them.

18 November 1974 – Ronnie DeFeo is charged with all six murders.

September 1975 – Ronnie DeFeo comes to trial. It is the longest trial ever held in Amityville. He tries to say the police beat him into confessing and that he didn't really kill his parents. He shows very little regret that his family are dead.

4 December 1975 – The Judge sentences Ronnie DeFeo to 150 years in prison. Ronnie DeFeo finally confesses to the massacre. "It just started," he said. "It went so fast . . . I just couldn't stop."

18 December 1974 – Meanwhile, a new family move into 112 Ocean Avenue – George Lutz and his wife, Kathleen. The children are from Kathleen's first marriage: two boys, Chris and Danny, and a little girl, Melissa – Missy for short.

The Lutzes know about the DeFeo murders – after all, that's how they got the house so cheaply – but they are not too bothered. Just to be safe they have their family priest, Father Frank Mancuso, come in to bless the house.

As Father Mancuso walks through the house sprinkling holy water, a deep voice says, "Get out!" Father Mancuso is puzzled but not worried . . . yet. Later that day his car almost crashes when the bonnet and door fly open. The car cannot be restarted.

He gets a lift from another priest – that priest later has a serious accident.

George Lutz discovers that much of the furniture of the dead DeFeos is in store since the massacre. He agrees to buy it. The house is returning to the way it was at the time of the gruesome murders.

The family dog is chained in a pen outside to guard the house. As darkness falls George hears the dog howling terribly. Something has scared it so badly that it tried to jump out of the pen and has almost strangled itself on the chain. George shortens the chain.

19 December 1974 – The family go to bed and sleep soundly – all except George Lutz, who wakens to an unexplained knocking at a quarter past three in the morning. This was the exact time at which the DeFeo family were murdered in their beds. George looks out of the window. The dog begins to bark furiously at something invisible down by the boathouse. George thinks he can see a shadowy shape vanishing into the boathouse. When he goes to investigate he finds the boathouse door swinging open in the freezing wind, yet he knows he closed it before he went to bed.

20 December 1974 – Things are starting to turn unpleasant for the Lutz family. George is waking at a quarter past three *every* morning. He is becoming short-tempered and hitting the children – something he has never done before. He is going for days without shaving or showering – something else he has never done. He is piling logs on the fire to warm himself during the day. The house is like an oven – but George is freezing.

22 December 1974 – Something strange happens to the toilets when they suddenly turn black with a stain that repeated scrubbing can't quite remove. A sickly-sweet perfume lingers in the air. When George goes to open a window to let out the smell, he sees it is covered with hundreds and hundreds of flies. Other windows are clear, but one window only is black with them. It is the window that faces the boathouse.

That night, at exactly a quarter past three, George is awakened by a crash. He hurries downstairs to find the front door torn open and hanging from one hinge.

24 December 1974 – Christmas Eve and Father Mancuso is ill with a raging temperature. George phones the priest and begins to tell him about the mysterious happenings. As Father Mancuso tries to give George a warning . . . the phone is mysteriously cut off. That evening the flies return to the window facing the boathouse.

George feels an urge to check the boathouse. As he turns back to the house he sees Missy staring out of the window at him. Behind the little girl is the face of a pig looking over her shoulder. The pig's eyes glow red. When he runs to her bedroom he finds the girl asleep.

25 December 1974 – George wakes – again at a quarter past three. His wife, Kathy, is sleeping with her head resting on her arms – just as the dead DeFeos were found. He touches her and she wakes screaming. "She was shot in the head! Mrs DeFeo was shot in the head! I heard the explosion!"

After Kathy has gone back to sleep the dog begins to bark. George slips outside. As he looks back to Missy's bedroom window he sees the little girl looking out at him. And, behind Missy's shoulder, is the face of that same pig staring out with glowing red eyes. When George checks her room, he again finds her lying asleep – face down with her head resting on her arms.

On Christmas Day, Missy begins to talk about her new friend – a pig called Jodie – but her brothers say the pig is just in her imagination. That night Kathy hears Missy talking to someone in her room. "Who are you talking to, Missy? An angel?"

"No, Mom, just my friend Jodie," the little girl tells her.

26 December 1974 – On Boxing Day a guest loses an envelope containing $1500, and the next day the Lutzes discover a hidden room behind a cupboard. The room has a sickly but familiar smell – it is the smell of blood.

Before New Year, George Lutz has begun to investigate the past of the house and its site. The local history association tell him it was near an American Indian camp for the sick, the mad and the dying – but the dead were never buried there because it was infested with demons.

1 January 1975 – Kathy Lutz sees the shape of a demon in the blazing log-fire. And, when the fire has died, the white shape of a horned head can be seen in the black soot of the chimney-back.

That night, a gale blows through the house and rips the bedclothes from George and Kathy's bed. The window facing the boathouse is open.

2 January 1975 – Mysterious footprints appear in the snow by the boathouse – hoofprints of the kind the devil is said to leave.

6 January 1975 – George wakes in the middle of the night. He looks across at his wife – she is not there. He switches on the light and sees her, floating in the air above the bed . . . but her face is that of a ninety-year-old woman. He drags her down by the hair, she awakes, looks at her face in the mirror and screams. Slowly her face returns to almost normal . . . but there are wrinkles in her face that weren't there before.

10 January 1975 – Kathy wakes to find her body covered in scratches. By the evening they have disappeared as mysteriously as they arrived. The curse of living in the house is affecting other parts of the family's life – George's business is heading towards bankruptcy.

11 January 1975 – This is one of the worst days yet. A storm smashes doors and windows while the rain floods in. The storm smashed trees in the garden of 112 Ocean Avenue – but not the trees in the rest of the street.

George and Kathy let the guard-dog into the house to see what it can sense. The dog refuses to go into Missy's room.

12 January 1975 – George wakes from a horrific nightmare. A hooded figure picked him up – the same figure the family had seen burned into the fireplace. The face emerged from the hood and George recognised it. It was his own face, but it was hideously torn in two!

As he woke from the dream, shaken, Missy tells him, "Daddy, come to my room. Jodie wants to talk to you."

"Who's Jodie?"

"Jodie's my friend. The biggest pig you ever saw."

George runs to the room. He can see no pig.

"There he is, Daddy!" Missy cries and points at the window. Two red eyes stare back in. No pig, not even a face. Just two red eyes.

"That's Jodie," the little girl cries. "He wants to come in!"

Kathy rushes past George, she picks up a chair and hurls it at the window. The window shatters; there is a squealing, pig-like scream of pain and the eyes vanish. There is nothing to be seen when they look through the broken window. But the squealing sound can be heard disappearing towards the boathouse.

13 January 1975 – Missy talks to Jodie under the table at breakfast.

"Who is this Jodie?" Kathy demands.

"He's an angel," Missy says. "He tells me about a little boy who used to live in my room. The little boy died, you know."

Missy's room was one where the DeFeos' young son had been murdered.

"Jodie says he's going to live here forever," Missy says proudly.

This is the final straw for the frightened Lutz family. They are sure that something is sharing the house with them. Something so horrible in smell and clammy touch that they can bear it no longer.

Their priest, Father Mancuso, advises them to "Let whatever's there have the place. Just go."

But, before they can leave, the storms return. The house grows hotter, though the heating is off – all except Missy's room which is freezing. George goes to open a window. He looks with disgust at the playroom door. Something green and slimy appears to be oozing through the door and into the hall. A jelly that has a mind of its own. The green slime begins to slither down the stairs. He manages to stop the flow by blocking the gap with towels.

14 January 1975 – George goes to bed, exhausted by his struggle against the slime. But he wakes to something climbing over his body – something with hooves.

The children wake screaming that some faceless creature has invaded their room. As George goes to investigate he sees that same huge hooded figure, blocking his way. It raises a finger and points at the man.

George gathers his family and orders them to get out. The Lutz family flee their house of horror. They have lived there just twenty-eight days.

George and his family move into the house of Kathy's mother. Peace at last . . . perhaps.

15 January 1975 – George is woken by his wife. "George! You were floating above the bed! We have to get out of this room!" She leads him out onto the landing. They stop. Coming up the stairs towards them is a trail of green-black slime . . .

Amityville – FACT FILE

Is the story true? Or was it invented by the Lutzes to get some publicity and make a lot of money from telling their story? Remember, George's business was failing! These are some of the facts that seem to support George and Kathy Lutz's story . . .

1. After the Lutzes moved out, a new family moved in. The son of the new owners slept in murderer Ronnie DeFeo's bedroom until he died at a tragically early age.

2. Jay Anson wrote a best-selling book on the case and sold the story to the makers of a very popular film. While he was writing the book some eerie things happened.

3. The manuscript of a few chapters was loaned to a woman . . . her house burst into flames and the only thing not damaged was the manuscript.

4. A man was driving with the manuscript in the boot of his car when the car slid into a deep, water-filled hole . . . and the only dry thing to be rescued next day was the manuscript.

5. The completed text was taken to the publisher by car . . . the car caught fire and all the engine bolts were found to be loose.

6.   Anson had a heart attack . . .

7.   . . . and his son was almost killed in a car crash.

8.   A photographer arrived at Jay Anson's house to photograph the author. For some reason his parked car burst into flames.

9.   Anson was so famous now that he earned one million dollars for his next book. Shortly after he received the million-dollar cheque, he died of a heart attack.

10.   Newspaper writer Paul Hoffman wrote the first article at the time of the strange happenings. He died some time later in strange circumstances.

11.   In the film, an actor called James Brolin played the part of George Lutz. He claimed he was hit by bad luck from the moment he started filming. His lift trapped him on the first day. On the second day he had been filming for one minute when he tripped and sprained an ankle. The delays cost the film company a fortune.

12.   The film-makers were so scared the story might be true that they refused to use 112 Ocean Avenue for the filming.

On the other hand, many people argue that the Amityville horror is nonsense because . . .

1. There are no witnesses to the strange happenings except for the family and their priest, who was feverish at that time with 'flu.

2. The claims that the house was built on an old Indian camp for the sick, the mad and the dying were simply not true. The Shinnecock Indians who lived in the region before white settlers arrived never had any such camp in any place.

3. The Parapsychology Institute of America (which investigates the supernatural) was called in by George Lutz . . . but then he suddenly cancelled the visit. Was he afraid that his claims would be proved false? The director of the Parapsychology Institute went ahead and personally investigated the house and the claims. He decided that the horror story was simply made up. (By then, of course, it was too popular a story. No one wanted to believe it was a fake!)

4. The next owners of the house, the Cromarty family, made a huge joke of the story. They were pestered by sightseers but didn't mind showing some people round the scenes of so-called horror. They even held Hallowe'en parties to tempt the demons out. Nothing unusual ever happened.

The Lutz family are alive and well. They moved to California where they were planning to write another book about their experiences.

THE GHOST OF THE RED·BARN

Can a ghost come back to earth and tell its relatives how it died? Some stories seem to prove that they can . . .

Polstead, Suffolk, England – 1827

The cottage was small, cold and very dark. It smelled of babies and dead moles. Mrs Ann Marten struck a light and lit a candle by the bedside. Her husband, John, snored deeply. "John," she hissed. The man groaned and turned his back to her. The mole-catcher was getting old, deaf and tired.

The woman pulled a shawl around her shoulders and put her lips closer to his ear. "John!" He smiled at some half-remembered dream but didn't wake. Somewhere in the shadows a sleeping child stirred.

Suddenly the chill air was split with a terrified scream. Mrs Ann Marten sat up in bed. A frightened child called out but her husband didn't move. The woman dug a sharp elbow into his ribs. "John, oh, John . . . I've had the most awful dream."

"Go back to sleep," her husband mumbled and blinked in the light of the flickering candle. "It isn't even daylight yet."

"No, John. You have to listen . . . it was a message from beyond the grave!"

The old man rubbed his eyes and struggled to sit up. "What you on about, my love?" he sighed.

"I dreamed about our Maria," she whispered. "She came to me and told me a dreadful story."

"Hah! Well what's all this rot about messages from beyond the grave?" the man grumbled. "Maria's alive and well."

"How do you know?" his wife asked.

"She got married to young William Corder and he took her off to live with him in London. She's safely asleep by now . . . like all good Christians should be," he added.

"No, John," Ann said and shuddered. "In the dream I saw

Maria covered in blood. She tried to speak to me. But all she could say was one word – murdered . . . by Corder!"

"That's three words," the man complained and settled down in the bed again.

"No, listen," the woman urged. "William Corder said he was taking her to London. He said he was going to marry her. But we haven't seen her since that night she left the cottage to meet him in the Red Barn."

"We've had letters," the man argued. But he was wide awake now and frowning.

"Only two or three – and in a strange handwriting," the woman argued.

"Hurt her hand, she said."

"So Corder said. He never wanted to marry our Maria. Him the squire's son and her a poor mole-catcher's daughter. I don't believe he ever went to London with Maria. I always thought that he wrote those letters himself."

The man didn't want to believe her. "So where is Maria if she's not in London with Corder?" he grumbled.

"If my dream were true then he . . . he murdered her!" the woman moaned.

"And what did he do with the body?" the old man asked and shivered again.

"I saw that in my dream too. He buried her in the Red Barn," Ann said. "I saw it in my dream. He murdered her and now her ghost is wandering the earth looking for justice."

"Who'll believe your word against the squire's son?" the man sighed. "What can you do?"

"Nothing," Ann sniffed. "Nothing a poor woman can do alone. But I did think you could go to the Red Barn and look."

The old man rubbed his eyes wearily. "First thing in the morning – well, second thing. Got to catch moles on the squire's orchard first thing. I'll do it second thing in the morning," he promised and turned over.

"No, John. Now!" the woman begged. "I'll never sleep again until I know."

"Dang me! I suppose that means I won't get any sleep either," the man grumbled as he fumbled in the dark for his trousers. He pulled on an old jacket and left the room. He paused at the front door to pick up his mole spud – a sharp wooden stake which he used to kill troublesome moles.

Within half an hour he'd gathered a group of villagers together and with lanterns and spades they set off for the old Red Barn on the top of the hill. With the owls screeching in the woods and the ragged black clouds drifting over the sickle moon, the idea of ghosts seemed more likely now. The villagers were a silent, frightened group as they tugged open the huge brown doors. Not a red barn at all – just a name given to it because of the way it caught the blood-red rays of the setting sun some evenings.

The barn was empty of hay at this time of the year. Another few weeks and the harvest would fill it. The lanterns on the floor caught the red eyes of the angry rats who squeaked and scuttled out of sight.

The floor was hard-packed earth. Too hard to dig it all. Men moved forward and prodded the ground with spades. Old John Marten used his mole spud – the spike clacked time and again against the hard floor. Then suddenly, the spud sank into a soft patch. "Ah!" the man gasped. He pulled out the spike. There was something sticky and evil-smelling on the end.

He stared at it. The villagers gathered around. "You want to go home while we dig?" one of the men asked.

The old man shook his head. Carefully the villagers scraped away the soft soil. The rats returned to watch curiously, their red eyes glinting in the lantern light. The shovels scraped away a crust of earth. Men knelt to scoop away the soft under-soil with their bare hands.

"Never did trust that William Corder," a woman muttered.

"Eyes too close together," her friend agreed. "A sure sign of wickedness . . . what's that?" she gasped and held her lantern to the ground.

"A scarf!" the man who was lifting soil out said as his hand tangled in a piece of fine material.

At last old John Marten spoke in a hoarse, agonised voice. "That's the scarf Maria was wearing the night she left!"

Someone led him away. They knew that Maria was still wearing that scarf. She had been buried with it round her neck.

"Just like Ann Marten's dream," a woman sighed. "God moves in mysterious ways."

"Amen," the villagers muttered as they slowly uncovered the body of poor Maria Marten. As they dragged the body clear of the shallow grave they found something else – a pistol. One of a pair of pistols. And the other belonged to William Corder.

Corder was traced to London and arrested. The trial was a sensation. The story of Maria Marten's murder in the Red Barn was turned into a play. Actors showed Corder killing Maria before the man had even been found guilty.

But the greatest sensation in the court and on the stage was Mrs Ann Marten's dream. It was a miracle. The ghost had returned to tell her mother of her murder. The body had been found where the ghost said it would be. Maria had returned from the grave to ask for justice and revenge.

If so, then she got it. Corder was hanged in front of a crowd of ten thousand people. That play, *Maria Marten* – or *The Murder in the Red Barn*, is still performed today.

Is this proof that ghosts really exist . . .?

Ghost of The Red Barn – FACT FILE

1.   Mrs Ann Marten wasn't Maria's mother. She was her stepmother, married to Maria's old father. Ann Marten wasn't much older than her step-daughter. When Maria was alive they argued bitterly. Why didn't the ghost appear in the dreams of her true blood relation, her father?

2.   One night in 1826 Maria told Mrs Marten that she was leaving to marry Corder. The next morning, Mrs Marten saw William Corder going towards the Red Barn with a pick-axe and a spade. Later that day Ann Marten asked Corder, "Where is Maria?" Corder replied, "She has gone to London to prepare for our wedding." Mrs Corder said this at the trial. But no one asked why Ann Marten wasn't suspicious then!

3.   William was writing letters to the Martens pretending they were written by Maria. But he was also enclosing money in the letters. Why?

4.   When the letters and the money stopped coming, Mrs Ann Marten had her amazing dream. Why did the "ghost" wait a year to appear?

Here's an explanation that fits the "facts" as we know them . . .

1.   Ann Marten was glad to see the back of Maria. She packed her off to meet Corder at the Red Barn at midnight. She didn't care if Maria lived or died – why should she?

2.   The next day she saw Corder with the pick-axe and spade and knew what had happened. Corder never wanted to marry the girl – he was a rich squire's son; she was a peasant – she could never mix in his society. But Maria was blackmailing him into marrying her – she was having his baby and that was not only a disgrace to Corder, it was also against the law if he failed to marry her. Mrs Marten must have known this. Mrs Marten didn't report her suspicions to the law officers – there was money to be made out of blackmailing Corder herself. "Pay me or I'll have the Red Barn searched."

3.   Corder went to London and faithfully paid the blackmail. But after a while he grew careless. He stopped paying and thought he was safe.

4.   Mrs Marten must have been furious. She couldn't go to the officers and say, "Corder's a murderer but he's been paying me to keep quiet," or she'd be hanged too.

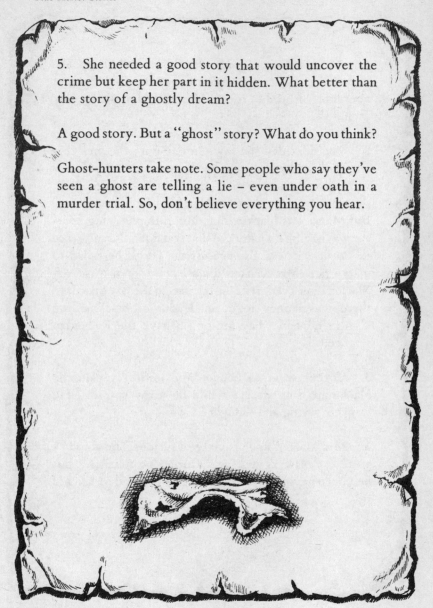

5.   She needed a good story that would uncover the crime but keep her part in it hidden. What better than the story of a ghostly dream?

A good story. But a "ghost" story? What do you think?

Ghost-hunters take note. Some people who say they've seen a ghost are telling a lie – even under oath in a murder trial. So, don't believe everything you hear.

Five Ways of Becoming a Ghost

1. Die without a proper burial. Without a proper burial you cannot rest in peace and are forced to wander the earth until your remains are laid to rest. Such ghosts are often heard to moan about their fate and, it is said, have to wait about nine hundred years if no one helps them.

2. Be a murder victim. Then you are compelled to haunt your killer or wander round and tell the world of your end until justice is done. Once your victim is caught and punished you can rest in peace.

3. Be thoroughly evil. If you're wicked on earth then you won't get into a respectable afterlife. You can hang around in "limbo" – neither life nor afterlife – until you have suffered enough for the evil you did when you were alive.

4. Listen out for your family calling you back. After you have gone to the afterlife your family may want to call you back. If the family uses a suitable "medium" (a person who has a "spirit" friend in the afterlife), then you may be recalled to earth to talk to your loved ones.

5. Die suddenly. If you are alive one moment then suddenly dead the next, you may not realise that you have died. Your spirit wanders round trying to carry on as if nothing has happened. It doesn't notice the body being carted off and may wonder why people run away when it approaches. Some battlefields are believed to be haunted by ghosts of this sort.

THE
WITCHeS
EXECUTION

Charles Walton was a strange old man. But did he deserve to die so horribly? And who killed him? And why could Britain's best detective not bring the killer to trial?

Lower Quinton, Warwickshire, England – 14 February 1945

"So what was the strangest case you ever investigated, Superintendent?" a young reporter asked.

The old policeman chuckled. "Ex-superintendent," he said. "I'm retired now."

Gillian Clifford leaned forward. She urged, "You'll always be the most famous detective in England, Superintendent. Everyone's heard of Fabian of the Yard. The cases you solved . . ."

"And the ones I didn't solve," Robert Fabian nodded.

"Like the Lower Quinton witch murder?" the girl said eagerly. "What's the truth about that?"

The retired policeman shook his head. "I can't tell you."

The girl's eyes grew large. "But you know?"

"I have no proof . . . you can't print my thoughts," he smiled.

The reporter closed her notebook. "I won't print anything. But I'd love to know. Tell me. Please."

The man sighed. He sucked on a cold pipe and looked out of the window into the winter-grey sky. "It was this time of year. Saint Valentine's day . . . but it wasn't a day for love. It was a day for death."

"And witchcraft," the girl reminded him.

"So they said. That was because of the old story, of course. Back in 1875 a man killed an old woman by pinning her to the ground with a pitchfork. He cut the sign of the cross into her throat. He said she was a witch and he had to kill her. That was just a few miles away from Lower Quinton."

"And you think Charles Walton was a witch and that was why he was killed in the same way seventy years later in 1945?" the reporter asked.

"I think nothing of the kind, young lady," Robert Fabian frowned. "I believe we were meant to think that!"

He closed his eyes and remembered. "Charles Walton was a strange old man. A bit of a loner, they said. Lived with his niece, Edith Walton. Hobbled around with a walking stick but he was still fit enough to work as a hedge-cutter when the weather was good enough."

"But he did claim to be a witch, didn't he?" the girl asked.

Fabian sucked the pipe again. "When he'd had a bit too much cider he said silly things . . . he claimed to be able to talk to animals!"

"Cider's a witch's brew, isn't it?" the girl asked.

Fabian of the Yard snorted. "I just deal in facts, Miss Clifford. What I discovered was that he had no enemies in the village. I learned that he set out from his cottage that Valentine's morning to cut the hedges of farmer Albert Potter. He had a pitchfork, a bill-hook for chopping the hedge . . . and his walking stick, of course. He told Edith that he'd be home about four."

"And that was the last time he was seen alive?"

"Not quite. Farmer Albert Potter said he saw someone cutting hedges at noon. He said the hedge-cutter was Charles Walton. The hedge-cutter was about a quarter of a mile from the farmhouse," Fabian said carefully.

"A quarter of a mile? Potter must have had good eyes!" the girl gasped.

"Potter said he saw the man's shirt sleeves as the man cut the hedge." Fabian stopped. He raised one eyebrow. "Old Charles Walton had been wearing a shirt with no sleeves."

"So Potter had seen the murderer!" the young reporter said

excitedly. The old policeman didn't reply. He simply looked out of the window and waited. Gillian frowned. What other explanation was there? Slowly she said, "Or Potter was lying?"

Fabian shrugged. "You can say that. I couldn't. Not without proof. But the facts were that Edith arrived home at six o'clock from work. The house was cold and dark and Uncle Charles was missing. She was worried straight away. She called on a neighbour, Harry Beasley, and they set off with a torch to Potter's farm. Potter told them where he'd seen the hedge-cutting going on and led them to the field. When they reached an old willow tree Potter stopped. He told Edith not to come any closer. Charles Walton was lying there . . . dead."

"Killed just like that old woman seventy years before," Gillian Clifford murmured. "A pitchfork pinning him to the ground and a sign of the cross cut into his throat." Suddenly a thought struck the reporter. "How old was Walton when he died?"

The policeman smiled. "Seventy-four."

"So he'd have been about four when the old witch was murdered. He must have known about it!" the girl said.

Fabian nodded. "That's what makes a good detective, Miss Clifford. Asking the right questions – making the right links. Of course, you're right! We checked back in the old police records for 1885 when Charles Walton was a boy." He paused.

"And you found something, didn't you!" Gillian cried.

"Nothing that helped us find his murderer," the ex-policeman sighed. "But something strange, I admit." He sucked on his pipe thoughtfully. "We discovered that a ploughboy had reported seeing a phantom black dog in the area. He'd seen it nine nights in a row on his way home from work . . ."

"And nine's the devil's number," the reporter put in.

"So they reckon," the man agreed. "On the ninth night the dog turned into a headless woman – the next day the ploughboy's sister, a fit and healthy woman, suddenly dropped dead."

"The black dog was a sign of a death in the family! A popular superstition. But what has that to do with Charles Walton?" she asked.

The ploughboy who reported the black dog was Charles Walton," Fabian said quietly.

"So he was into witchcraft!" the girl insisted.

The man shrugged. "All I know is that the stories scared the local people – especially when we found a black dog hanging from a tree near the site of the murder."

"So you found nothing?"

"We found no reason why Charles Walton had to die. No one seemed to have a motive to kill a quiet old man. We did find fingerprints on the handle of the pitchfork – they belonged to farmer Albert Potter. He said he'd tried to pull the fork from the body when he found it . . . but it wouldn't come out."

"Surely he could have managed!" Gillian frowned.

Fabian leaned forward and pointed at the girl with the stem of his pipe. "Miss Clifford, it took two strong policemen to remove that pitchfork. It had gone clean through Charles Walton and deep into the ground."

Gillian shuddered. "So it had to be someone strong. His niece couldn't have done it? I mean, she'd be the one to get his cottage when he died, wouldn't she?"

The man shook his head. "She was at work all day . . . and you're right. It took someone very strong, almost certainly a man."

"Did Walton have any money?" the girl asked suddenly.

"Well, he was very careful with money. He had a bit tucked away. But he wouldn't have had any on him when he was killed. All he had was a pocket watch. And that was missing."

"He wouldn't have been killed for a pocket watch," the reporter said.

"No. And that was found in Walton's garden years later. No, we couldn't find a motive that would hold up in court. That legend of the black dog scared everyone into silence. We got no real help from the villagers, and after a police car knocked over and killed a black dog, people were afraid to help. Seemed we were cursed. Some of them became quite ill after we visited them!" the ex-policeman grumbled.

"So you still say the case had nothing to do with witchcraft?"

"I do know that I was near the scene of the murder one day when a large black dog ran past me. A farm boy appeared straight after. I asked him if he was looking for his black dog. He nearly choked with fright and ran away," Fabian said, slowly shaking his head.

"So who did it, superintendent?" Gillian asked.

He leaned forward again. "Work it out. Who could have done it?"

The reporter frowned. "Farmer Albert Potter," she said. "But what was his motive?"

"We'll come to that in a moment. Just tell me how he could have done it and I'll tell you why he'd want to do it."

Gillian nodded. "Walton was working in Potter's fields. Potter knew he was there because he told the inquest. But he couldn't have seen him a quarter of a mile away. He saw him close to . . . and thought up the story about the shirt sleeves." She paused. "He killed Walton with the pitchfork . . . he was a farmer so he'd probably be strong enough to pin him down like that. Potter went back to his farm. Walton's niece called at Potter's farm later that night and Potter led them straight to the body. And, of course, Potter's fingerprints were on the pitchfork."

Fabian smiled. "Very good. Not enough to charge the man,

but enough to suspect him."

"And the motive?"

"Only suspicion there. No proof at all. But remember old Walton's bit of money he had tucked away. I can tell you that Potter's farming business was not doing well at the time of the murder . . . and he was fond of gambling on the horses. He was definitely short of money. Edith Walton reckoned that Uncle Charles had loaned a lot of money to Potter – all cash, of course. No proof of the loans once Walton was dead."

"I see!" Gillian said eagerly. "On the day of the murder Walton went round to Potter's farm to cut hedges and to ask for some of his money back. The two men argued. Potter didn't have the money. They fought. Potter snatched the pitchfork and killed old Walton!"

"So why would he cut a cross in his throat after the old man was dead?" Fabian asked.

The reporter closed her eyes and tried to concentrate. "When Charles Walton was dead, Potter remembered the old legend of the witch-killing. He didn't want people to look for a real murder motive like money. He wanted to fool the police into looking for a witch-craft murderer!"

"Very good, Miss Clifford. Of course we can't prove any of it. And while Potter's still alive, *you* can't write what we think. But I'm absolutely certain that old Walton wasn't the victim of black magic or black dogs. It was something much simpler – and much more boring, I'm afraid."

The reporter nodded. "Plain and simple greed."

Valentine's Day Murder – FACT FILE

1.   Warwickshire had a reputation for witchcraft in the 16th and 17th centuries.

2.   An old legend tells of a Warwickshire hill, Meon Hill, being the work of the Devil. The Devil took a huge clod of earth and threw it at a new abbey in Evesham in the eighth century. Saint Egwin used prayer to protect the abbey and the clod fell short. It became Meon Hill. The body of old Charles Walton was found at the foot of Meon Hill.

3.   The appearance of a black dog is a sign of the Devil being in the area. Some people believe that the Devil can take the shape of a black dog.

4.   The cross shape (cut into the throat) was a Christian sign to stop the Devil from raising a witch from the dead.

5.   The iron of the pitchfork was considered a strong magic force which kept evil spirits away from the body. By pinning the "witch" to the ground those evil spirits couldn't fly off with the body.

A DREAM OF DEATH

Usually, sudden, violent death comes as a complete surprise – but sometimes the victim simply knows how he will die . . .

Washington DC, USA – 14 April 1863

President Abraham Lincoln should have been the happiest man in the USA. For years, the war between the Northern states and the Southern states had raged. Now it was all but over, yet Lincoln was strangely sad.

He sat with his wife Mary and his friend Ward Hill Lamon drinking tea late one night. "You're in a serious mood tonight, Abraham," Lamon said.

The President nodded slowly. The years of struggle had weakened him. He was thin and frail. His black hair and beard straggled untidily. "It's strange how much there is written in the Bible about dreams."

The President leaned forward and rested his elbows on his knees. "If we believe the Bible then we must accept that, in the old days, God and his angels came to people in their sleep and gave them messages through their dreams. Today people think that dreams are foolish."

He fell silent and his dark, sunken eyes stared at the carpet.

"So do you believe in dreams?" Mary asked quietly.

After a while her husband answered. "I can't say that I do . . . but I had one the other night that has haunted me ever since."

Mary Lincoln was a short, plump woman who was usually pale. Now she turned a ghostly white. "You frighten me! What was that dream?"

The tall man sighed and twisted his long, thin hands as he told of his dream. "About ten days ago I went to bed very late. I was exhausted and soon fell into a deep sleep and then began to dream. And in the dream there seemed to be a death-like stillness all around me. Then I heard sobbing as if a number of people were weeping. I dreamed I left my bed and wandered downstairs.

"There I heard the same pitiful sobbing, but the people who were crying seemed to be invisible. I wandered from room to room but there was no living person in sight, only the mournful sounds of distress as I passed along. It was light in all the rooms. I recognised each room, but where were all the people who were grieving as if their hearts would break?

"I was puzzled and worried. What could be the meaning of all this? I walked on until I reached the East Room, which I entered. There I met with a sickening surprise. In front of me was a coffin, and in it was a corpse dressed in burial clothes – its face covered. Around the coffin were soldiers who guarded it; there was a crowd of people, some gazing mournfully at the corpse, and some weeping pitifully.

"I asked one of the soldiers who the dead person was. He told me it was the President, and he had been killed by an assassin! There came a loud burst of crying from the crowd which woke me from my dream. I slept no more that night and, though it was only a dream, I have been strangely troubled ever since." The President fell silent. The story was over.

"That's horrid!" Mary gasped. "I'm glad I don't believe in dreams or I'd be in terror for ever more!" and she hurried off to the comfort of her bed.

But Lamon lingered. "Abraham, perhaps you should be more careful. Don't go out after dark, not even with a guard."

The President gave a weary smile. "Why would anyone wish to assassinate me? And if he did then he could do it any time, day or night, if he was ready to die in the attempt. It is nonsense! What man would be ready to give his life for mine?"

John Wilkes Booth was perhaps the most famous actor in America at that time. Tall, handsome and popular, Booth loved acting and all the fame that went with it. But it still wasn't enough. Booth wanted a greater fame. He wanted fame that would last forever. He wanted to be remembered for some great deed, and remembered long after he was dead.

John Wilkes Booth lived in the Northern states but, during the war, his support was for the Southern states where he'd been born. One man had brought the war about and Wilkes Booth hated him like poison; one man had been to blame for the defeat of the South and Wilkes Booth hated him so much he wanted to kill him . . . even if it cost him his own life! That one man was Abraham Lincoln.

Wilkes Booth plotted and planned but not many men were as willing to risk their lives to see Lincoln dead. He knew he would have to carry out the assassination alone. Still, one man should not have been able to murder a well-guarded President. He would need a lot of luck.

The people wanted to see the President who had helped them win the war. The President didn't much enjoy the theatre, but a visit would make his wife happy and please the people who wanted him to appear in public. He decided to visit Ford's Theatre to see a comedy play.

The President wouldn't sit with the crowds in the ordinary seats. He would sit in the best seats in Ford's Theatre – a box at the side of the stage.

It was private; he could only be seen from the audience if he leaned forward. It was safe; the back door to the box should be locked, and to reach that door a killer would have to pass through a white door which would be guarded by an armed policeman.

John Wilkes Booth was an actor, so he knew Ford's Theatre like he knew his own home. The loathsome President Lincoln was going to walk straight into the killer's chosen den. That afternoon he began his planning.

First, the play. Booth walked into the theatre. "Good afternoon," the stage-hands whispered, pleased to see the famous man. They led him to a seat where he could watch the actors practising.

Booth watched the play and took note of the time as each scene came and went. Actor Henry Hawk was on stage. Alone on stage. Booth reckoned this would be a good time to kill the President. Afterwards, he could jump from the President's box, run across the stage, and only Henry Hawk would stand between him and freedom.

Booth looked at his watch. The play had run for two and a quarter hours. When the real performance was on that night then this scene would be playing at a quarter past ten. That was the time that the President would die.

Henry Hawk looked off the side of the stage and called after a fussy old character, "You sockdologising old mantrap!" That line would get a good laugh.

No one noticed as Booth slipped from his seat and wandered up the stairs and towards the empty box seats. He went through the white door. He found a piece of wood and made it fit between the white door and the wall behind. Once he'd escaped through there, the spar would jam the door shut.

He tried the door to the President's box, looking closely at the lock. It was broken! Booth couldn't believe his luck.

The actor took a small penknife out of his pocket and bored a hole in the door to the box. From there he could see the back of the chair where the hated Lincoln would sit. The President's special chair – a rocking-chair.

He stood in the shadow at the back of the box and watched the actors rehearsing. The stage was just three metres below. An easy jump to freedom.

John Wilkes Booth walked out of the theatre. All he had to do was wait.

Darkness began to fall. Lincoln left for the theatre. As his daytime guard, Crooks, left the White House Lincoln said, "Goodbye, Crooks." The guard wondered why the President had said "Goodbye" and not "Goodnight".

The night guard arrived, late as usual. And a hundred miles to the south of Washington, Ward Hill Lamon looked up at the gloomy sky and worried about his friend the President.

He hoped that Lincoln would take notice of his warning and not go out. Lamon suddenly remembered another strange vision that Lincoln once had. The President had been lying on a couch when he glanced up at a mirror. He saw two reflections: one bright and glowing, the other ghastly as death. "I see the meaning, Lamon. I will have two periods of office as President. The first will be healthy but death will come before the end of the second."

Tonight Lincoln was nearing the end of his second period in office. Lamon shuddered. He would never forgive himself if anything happened to his friend while he was away.

As the clocks crept round to a quarter past ten, the moon rose. Farmers in the western states swore that when the moon rose that night it was the colour of blood.

John Wilkes Booth walked through the front entrance to the theatre.

"Ticket, please?" the sleepy booking clerk asked.

Booth put on a joking act of shock. "You will not want a ticket from me!"

The clerk recognised the great actor and grinned. "Sorry, Mr Booth. Go on in!"

The actor had a small, one-shot pistol up his sleeve and a large knife in his belt.

He climbed the stairs and practised the most important line he had ever had to learn. The line that would tell the guard at the white door this lie: "Message for the President!"

Booth came slowly down the side steps of the darkened theatre, the steps that led to the President's box. He reached the white door. The guard's chair stood empty. Police Officer John F Parker had been there until ten o'clock. He hadn't been able to see the play from there and had grown bored. He left the theatre at the interval and went to a local inn for a drink. The police officer never returned.

So Booth's luck was in. He didn't need his well-rehearsed words. He opened the white door and wedged it shut behind him with the piece of wood. Booth crept to the door of the box and put an eye to the hole he had bored in the corner. Actors' voices drifted up from the stage below. As he grew used to the dimness of the box he could make out the rocking-chair. And the shape of the detested Lincoln's head appeared above the high back.

Booth's hand reached for the pistol. With his other hand he slowly turned the handle of the unlocked door and slid through as silently as settling dust. The President's head was a metre away. The assassin in the shadows raised the pistol. As the hand with the pistol came ever closer, the President's eyes were fixed on the stage. One by one the actors and actresses made their exits. Finally, only Harry Hawk was left.

On stage the actor cried, "You sockdologising old mantrap!"

They were the last words the sixteenth President of the United States ever heard. The audience roared with laughter ... so loud it drowned the roar of John Wilkes Booth's pistol. The single bullet smashed into the President's head. It entered just behind his left ear and came to rest behind his right eye.

"Revenge for the South!" Booth cried.

Mrs Lincoln turned and looked at the handsome young man who'd appeared in her box. She wondered why her husband didn't move. Slowly the cloud of gunsmoke drifted towards her and the gaslights of the stage glinted on the killer's knife.

Over the screams of laughter from the audience came the screams of Mary Lincoln. The President's dream of death had come true.

Booth jumped onto the stage and broke his leg. He managed to escape but was later found hiding in a barn. He was shot.

"What man would be ready to give his life for mine?" President Lincoln had wondered. The answer was John Wilkes Booth.

Lincoln was carried from Ford's Theatre to a house across the road. He died the next morning.

The Assassination of Lincoln – FACT FILE

Almost a hundred years later, President John Kennedy was shot by an assassin. Many people see startling similarities between the two assassinations.

1.   President Lincoln was succeeded by his Vice-President – a man called Johnson . . . President Kennedy was succeeded by *his* Vice-President – a man called Johnson.

2.   Lincoln's killer, John Wilkes Booth, had a name of three words with fifteen letters in all . . . Kennedy's killer, Lee Harvey Oswald, also had a name of three words with fifteen letters in all.

3.   Lincoln died by a bullet in the back of the head as he sat next to his wife in the Ford Theatre . . . Kennedy died by a bullet in the back of the head as he sat next to his wife in a Ford car.

4.   Lincoln's killer shot the President in a theatre and hid in a storeroom (a barn) . . . Kennedy's killer shot the President from a storeroom and hid in a theatre.

The Legend of Lincoln – FACT FILE

Lincoln's dream of death was reported by Lamon as a miraculous warning – but Lamon did not tell this story until some time after the assassination. Over the years many stories grew up around Lincoln and his links with the supernatural. It is said that . . .

1. Lincoln went to a spiritualist who was in touch with the dead. It was she who told him that the spirits wanted him to free the slaves in the Southern states. He took her advice and it was this action that started the American Civil War.

2. A woman went to a spiritualist photographer. His business was taking pictures of the living which turned out to have images of the dead on them after they had been developed. When the woman's picture was printed, the image of Abraham Lincoln appeared to be looking over her shoulder. The woman then revealed her true name – Mary Lincoln, the President's widow! BUT . . . the photographer, Mumler, was later accused of being a trickster! Some of his photos were shown to be fakes.

3. There have been many reports of Lincoln's ghost being seen in the White House over the years.

– Mrs Mary Lincoln was the first to report seeing her husband's ghost. BUT . . . Mrs Lincoln was a nervous, hysterical woman with a vivid imagination. She later became seriously mentally ill.

– Queen Wilhelmina of the Netherlands was staying at the White House when she heard a knocking at the bedroom door. She opened it and fell to the floor in a faint. She later told President Roosevelt that she had seen the figure of President Lincoln standing there.

– President Roosevelt never saw the ghost himself but once said that when he was alone in the Blue Room he could often feel the comforting presence of Lincoln's spirit.

– President Harry H Truman said that he had been woken several times by a rapping on his bedroom door while he was at the White House. Truman, unlike Queen Wilhelmina, never saw a ghost.

– Lincoln's appearances have often been announced by a loud, booming laugh for which he was famous.

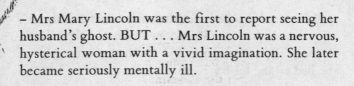

– A terrified maid reported to President Roosevelt's wife that she had seen President Lincoln in the Lincoln Room; the ghostly figure had been sitting on the edge of the bed taking his boots off.

THE
GHOST IN THE
L·I·F·T

Can a ghost see into the future and warn you of a disaster? Some people believe so. And for many years this story has gone around which seems to prove it.

County Offaly, Ireland – 1883

Lord Dufferin led a busy life, travelling the world in the service of his country. He'd completed six years as the Governor-General of Canada. But now he needed a break.

He had to write a report – an important report for the British government. So he decided that a trip to Ireland would give him the peace he needed. He didn't get it – instead he got something much more valuable. An experience that would save his life ten years later.

Lord Dufferin was tired. The great house near Tullamore in Ireland was silent now – even the servants had gone to bed. He took the candle he'd been working by and lit his way to bed. Not long after he laid his head on the pillow, he drifted into a calm, deep sleep. Until . . .

He awoke with a start. Lord Dufferin didn't know what had woken him. He only knew that it was terrifying. A dream? No, it wasn't a dream. A noise! That was it. He'd been woken by a noise. As he strained his ears he heard it again. And this time he wasn't dreaming. A noise outside on the lawn. The jangle of a horse's harness and the creak of a carriage wheel. But the sound that had chilled him was the soft wailing that was half-human, half-animal.

He was suddenly wide awake – and terrified.

A horse and carriage had no right to be clattering over the lawn of the great house. It belonged on the drive at the front. And what was it doing there in the middle of the night?

In the dim glow of his night-light he found his slippers and tiptoed over to the window. Moon shadows drifted over the silver-green lawn. And from the shadows a man staggered. Staggered under the weight of a huge box on his back.

Lord Dufferin threw open the window to ask the man what was going on. At that moment he realised that the box on the man's back was no ordinary box . . . it was a coffin. He ran across to the man and called him to stop. The stranger raised his head and glared.

"What are you doing here? And what's in that box?" demanded Lord Dufferin.

The stranger's face twisted into an evil leer of pure hated, but he stayed silent. After a few moments he turned to walk back to his carriage.

"Stop!" Lord Dufferin cried and ran after the man, snatching at his arm. But Lord Dufferin's hand seemed to pass clean through that arm.

The stranger threw the coffin onto the carriage where another coffin lay. There was a space left on the carriage wide enough for a third coffin. The strange man turned and snarled at Lord Dufferin. He spoke for the first and only time. "Room for one more, sir, room for one more."

His Lordship boldly ran to grab the man and force him to explain. As he did so the man vanished into the moonlit air. Still shaking, Lord Dufferin returned to his room and made careful notes of what he had seen.

Next morning he read the notes over breakfast to some of his friends who lived locally. "Never been a report of a ghost in this house before," he was told.

"And there's no one in Tullamore who fits the description of this man," someone added with a shake of the head.

"Perhaps it really was just a nightmare. You're over-tired from all that work," a kind friend suggested. "Forget it."

And in time that's just what Lord Dufferin did. Pushed it to the back of his mind, got on with his important work and forgot the man with the coffin.

Almost . . .

Ten years passed. Lord Dufferin became Ambassador to France. He was invited to a glittering reception at the Grand Hotel in Paris.

When he arrived he found the hotel was crowded. And the reception was on the top floor of the hotel. The lifts were very popular that day.

"You could always walk up the stairs," a friend told him.

"Four flights!" Lord Dufferin gasped. "At my age? No," he chuckled. "I'll just be patient and wait for this lift," he said, joining the queue.

The doors slid open and the guests streamed forwards. The lift was full in seconds.

"Better luck next time," someone sighed.

And next time the lift arrived there was indeed a space. The lift looked full so Lord Dufferin stepped back. But the lift attendant thrust his head around the door and looked the ambassador in the eye.

Lord Dufferin stepped back with a cry as he saw the man. The same ugly, evil face of the man he'd seen carrying a coffin in that vision just ten years before. "Room for one more, sir," the lift man leered. "Room for one more."

Lord Dufferin shook his head dumbly and staggered back to a chair where he shook with the same fear that had shaken him all those years ago. Weakly, he pushed himself to his feet and walked across to the manager's office.

"Can I have a word?" he asked politely. He didn't know what he wanted to say. Some sort of question about the man . . . or perhaps some sort of warning.

"Of course, monsieur," the manager smiled. "How can I help you?"

As Lord Dufferin struggled to find the right words a waiter rushed through the door and yelled. "Come quickly!" he panted. "The lift!"

"The lift? What's wrong with the lift?" Lord Dufferin whispered.

"Oh, monsieur! The cable snapped when it reached the top. It crashed back down. We fear the people are all dead."

And Lord Dufferin knew that, but for that night at Tullamore, he too would have been a victim of that lift disaster. The vision had saved his life.

The Ghost in the Lift – FACT FILE

1.   Lord Dufferin held his title from 1862 until he died in 1902.

2.   The first published report of Lord Dufferin's ghost in the lift story did not appear till 1920 – eighteen years after his death and twenty seven years after the supposed crash. Why did the world have to wait so long to hear this incredible story? If it were true then it would have been a newspaper sensation back in 1893, wouldn't it?

3.   A lift accident did occur in the Grand Hotel . . . but that was in 1878 – five years before Lord Dufferin's dream and fifteen years before the story says it happened. When the accident did happen there was no reception at the hotel, Lord Dufferin was in Canada at the time – and only one lady died. There is no report of an accident in 1893. How do these facts tie in with the story?

4.   The writer of the first story had the facts told to him shortly after his story appeared in print. He never bothered to change the story, however, and many people have retold the same story without bothering to mention the mistakes. Why didn't the 1920 writer bother to check the facts before he printed the story?

So What Really Happened?

1.   Lord Dufferin was a lively and popular person. After dinner parties he would entertain friends with stories. When the candles burned low and the night winds howled, what better than a ghost story to thrill his listeners?

2.   One of Lord Dufferin's favourite ghost stories was about a woman who answered the door, only to find a hearse waiting outside. The ugly undertaker asked if the woman was ready to go with him. She refused . . . as you would . . . and slammed the door. The ugly man turned up many years later as a lift attendant. Remembering the old vision, the woman refused the lift – it crashed and she was saved.

3.   Every time Lord Dufferin told this story he changed it a little. One evening, to entertain a bored nephew, he told the story as if it had happened to him! But the young nephew believed every word and in years to come repeated the story and said that he knew for a fact it had happened to Lord Dufferin.

4.   So the spooky story became a fact in the eyes of many listeners. Twenty years later it was published in a book, and proved to be full of factual mistakes. Why didn't the writer change the story when he discovered this? Because it made a better story the way it was told – and good ghost stories make money. Other writers

copied the story and, of course, swore that it must be true simply because they had read it. When some people hear a good story, they like to believe it. But when that same story is put in a book, then nearly everyone believes it!

5.   If you are looking for the truth about ghosts, then the message is simple: *don't* believe everything you read!

FIVE EXPLANATIONS FOR GHOSTS

1.   **Spirits of the Dead** – Every human has a body (flesh and blood and bones and so on) and a spirit. The body will wear out eventually but the spirit can live on without the body. It may then return to relive its life or to tell its story to any living person who cares to listen.

2.   **Energy Recordings** – When something dramatic or violent occurs with humans, a lot of energy is released. This energy leaves an "imprint" in the air – the way people can make an imprint on video-tapes. This "recording" can then "replay" itself and the characters in the violent event can be seen time and again in the same place.

3.   **Imagination** – Human beings have a very powerful imagination and can't always control it. If you are in a dark and lonely place then you might be terrified of seeing a ghost. This makes your brain "create" a ghost in front of your eyes. It seems real at the time – but then so does a dream when you are asleep. Ghosts may be waking dreams.

4.   **Fraud** – People lie about seeing ghosts – it makes a good story to impress friends. Some people enjoy scaring others with conjuring-type tricks that create the sounds and images of ghosts. And some can make a lot of money out of lying and cheating with ghosts.

5. **Space-Time Warps** – Our universe is not solid – it just looks that way to our simple brains. In fact there are many universes all existing side-by-side in the same space. Sometimes the fabric of our universe cracks for a moment and we see into another time and another place. So if someone walks across a field in another universe – in our universe that may be a house. The ghost walks clean through the wall of our house because it isn't there for him. Or maybe it is not a space-warp but a time-warp. The past, the present and the future are all happening at the same time. Sometimes we move "sideways" in time instead of forwards and see something happen in the past or the future.

THE
VaNISHING
VILLAGE

People have been fascinated by life in other parts of the universe ever since humans first looked up and saw the stars. Sometimes alien life seems the only explanation for the strange and horrific occurrences on our own planet. Occurrences like that in a village in Canada earlier this century . . .

Lake Anjikuni, Canada – Winter 1930

The sky was purple-black and endless. The stars burned cold as splinters of ice. The wind seemed to be even colder. It stung the faces of the two men as they staggered home under the weight of the dead animals they had slung over their backs.

Ice began to form in the beard of the old man, Armand Laurent. His son, Raoul, stumbled behind and cursed the dark that made him trip on the tree roots. A mile to go and the shelter of the cabin. Ten minutes walking and ten more minutes for a fire to thaw his aching eyes.

At first Raoul thought he was seeing things. He thought his eyes were playing tricks as the trail turned blood-orange in front of him. But his father stopped and looked around too. Even his father's frosted beard was sparkling in the light.

Armand was looking over his son's shoulder. Raoul had never seen his father show fear. The old man's eyes were wide and glittering with terror now.

Raoul dropped the frozen carcasses on the snow-covered path and turned stiffly. He blinked up into the sky. The stars had vanished. Another light, much brighter, had swallowed them – a brilliant bar of light as bright as a glowing-hot poker.

The light hung in the sky about twenty miles to the north. Slowly at first, then faster, it began to move. It began to move towards the trappers. Raoul snatched at the dead animals and stumbled down the trail. His father tumbled after him.

They didn't stop until they reached the safety of the log

cabin. But by that time the light had shrunk to a star-sized dot, then vanished. Armand slammed the door and bolted it fast, as if the bolt could keep the terror out.

Next morning they rose and ate. Then they skinned the trapped animals. They went about their lives like two men walking in their sleep. They didn't speak about what they had seen.

Three days later their silent work was disturbed by a knocking at the door.

The man seemed to be knocking on the door of the wooden cabin with something metal. "Mr Laurent! Royal Canadian Mounted Police here! Could I see you, sir?"

Armand pulled back the bolts, lifted the latch and squinted out of the gloomy cabin into the snow-bright evening light.

"Good evening, Mr Laurent," the young Mountie said. His face was red with the frosted air, and ice was dusting his black hat and overcoat. He stamped his feet on the frozen ground and tried to smile a stiff grin. His weary horse blew clouds of steam into the still air.

"Er . . . evening," Armand nodded. His sharp blue eyes looked down at the metal object in the Mountie's hand. It was a gun. He started back.

The Mountie looked down and laughed. "Just used it as a door knocker. You don't seem to have one!"

"Don't need one," Armand replied gruffly. "Don't get many visitors when you're twenty miles from the nearest town."

The Mountie nodded and looked past the old man into the warm darkness of the cabin. "I was just wondering if you could help me," he said.

"Help you with your enquiries? Is that it?" Armand asked sharply. "Look, mister, I'm just a poor trapper, catching and skinning animals for a living. I haven't broken any laws!"

The Mountie shook his head wearily. "No, no, Mr Laurent.

Nothing like that. I'm just not too sure of the trail ahead and I thought you might be able to help me. They reckon you know every inch of trail for a hundred miles around, sir."

"Yep," Armand nodded and couldn't help relaxing a little. "Where are you headed?"

"Lake Anjikuni, sir."

"An Eskimo village? You're half a day's ride from there. You'll never make it before nightfall, son."

The Mountie sighed. "You reckon I could stable my horse here for the night?"

Old Armand looked doubtful. He rubbed his thin grey beard. "I'd pay, of course," the Mountie said.

Armand's face lightened. "Raoul!" he called over his shoulder. "Take this gentleman's horse and put it in the barn. Give it oats, hay and fresh water!"

Raoul hurried to obey his father as the old man led the way into the log cabin and the warmth of the stove. With the horse stabled and a good meal inside him the young mounted policeman seemed keen to talk to the Laurents. "Duvall's my name. Sergeant Alain Duvall."

"And what brings you out here?" Raoul asked. "We don't see many Mounties round these parts."

"We had a report from a trapper in this area – guy called Joe Labelle. You know him?"

"Of course. We sometimes work together," Armand said.

"Seems Joe Labelle came into town yesterday with some crazy story about people going missing from the Eskimo village by Lake Anjikuni. I was sent out to investigate. Took me longer to get here than I reckoned. You'll know Lake Anjikuni, Mr Armand?"

"Sure. The Eskimo hunt and trap and trade just like me."

"And you don't know anything about missing people?" the Mountie asked.

"No-o," the trapper said uneasily.

"They probably went out to see the lights," Raoul said quickly. It was the first time the young man had admitted he'd seen anything.

His father tried to give him a warning glance. It was too late. "Lights?" the Mountie asked.

"Lights in the sky," Raoul explained. "Didn't Joe Labelle tell you about them?"

The old trapper sighed. "You'll probably think we're crazy. It happens, you know. Men out here, alone, start to see things."

The Mountie leaned forward and the red light of the stove gleamed in his eager eyes. "Just tell me what you saw, Mr Laurent."

"It was about three days ago . . . or three nights rather. We'd just emptied the last traps on the ridge and were coming in for supper. We were in the trees on the slope when we saw an orange glow."

"We thought the cabin was on fire," Raoul cut in. "Nothing else round here to make a light like that."

"But we could see it was a light in the sky. It was huge! Never seen anything like it before," Armand said. "Hope I never see anything like it again!"

"What shape was this thing?" Sergeant Duvall asked.

"Cigar," Raoul said.

"Cylinder," Armand said at the same moment.

The father and son looked at each other, annoyed. "To tell the truth it changed as it moved," Raoul said.

"So this bright light was moving? Which direction?" the Mountie asked.

"Across the sky to the north," the trapper said.

"North? Isn't that the direction of Lake Anjikuni?"

"That's right," Armand nodded.

The Mountie rose to his feet and stretched. "If you guide me to the village tomorrow I'll make sure the Mounted Police pay you double," he said. "Mind if I just take this bed over here?"

"Fine!" Armand said and found some blankets for his guest.

The next morning was dull and a freezing wind came down from the north. The three men had to ride into it. After two weary hours they crested the ridge that overlooked the slate-grey lake and the huddle of wooden houses.

The old trapper's sharp eyes narrowed and he squinted through his red-rimmed eyes. "I've never seen anything like that before," he breathed.

"Something wrong, Mr Laurent?" the Mountie asked.

Armand could only shake his head with wonder for the first few minutes. "Nothing there!"

The Mountie gave an uncomfortable laugh. "There's the village there."

"But it's deserted," Armand said.

"We're over a mile away, Mr Laurent. How can you tell?"

The old man gave a bad-tempered wave of his hand. "Not one whiff of smoke from any of those chimneys. And the wind's coming from that direction. We'd hear them from here! The sled dogs are always barking."

The Mountie shrugged. "I know Joe Labelle said there were people missing. I didn't know he meant everyone had gone!"

"They can't have," Raoul said. "There's over twelve hundred people live in that village."

"Let's look," Armand said shortly and led the way down the slippery trail into the village. Ten minutes later they reached the first house.

The Mountie jumped off his horse and hammered on the first door. There was no answer. "Must be out on some hunting trip," he suggested.

Armand Laurent shook his head. "There's a rifle leaning in the doorway . . . no Eskimo would ever leave the village without it. Even if he wasn't hunting he might meet some bears on the trail."

The Mountie put his shoulder to the door and pushed. The weak lock splintered. The house was as cold inside as it was out. A leather coat lay on a bed. It was half-mended. Two bone needles lay beside it. "They must have left in a hurry," he said.

Raoul was exploring the second room. "A pot of stew in here. Caribou by the look of it!"

"I could use a bite," his father said.

"Not of this stew. It's been cold for days." Raoul put a hand to the ashes of the fireplace and shook his head. "No fire here for three days at least."

"Three days?" the Mountie said, coming through the doorway behind him. "Three days since you saw those lights, wasn't it Mr Laurent?"

Armand just nodded. "They left in a hurry. Didn't bother eating before they went . . . and they didn't take the over-land trail or they'd have taken their rifles."

"Maybe they got scared by the lights and crossed the lake," the Mountie suggested.

The three men left the house and crunched down the deserted, snow-covered street. No human tracks broke the crisp white mantle of fresh snow. They turned towards the lake edge and stopped before they even reached the small wooden landing stages. Boats and kayaks crowded the mooring posts. "Must be very near every boat in the village there," Armand said. "Twelve hundred people didn't leave across the lake."

Sergeant Duvall looked up at the snow-filled clouds. "We got time to check the trail out of the village?" he asked.

"This way," Armand said. He led the way through the village. There was no sound, no movement, no warmth in a place that had been overflowing with life just a week before.

They found the dog sleds first. They had been tied to the trees on the edge of the town. Then they had been abandoned. The dogs had died of the cold and hunger. The Mountie was sickened by the sight. "I'd better get back and report this," he said. "If we leave now I could get back to base before night."

But Armand was looking back at the village. One field on the edge was not lying smoothly under the snow. It was pitted with deep trenches that were only half-filled by the drifts. He walked towards it silently, leading his horse. When Sergeant Duvall reached his side he was standing staring at the field.

"What is it, Mr Laurent?"

Armand pointed at the empty troughs. "It's not just the living that have gone from the village," he croaked. "This here was the graveyard. And it looks like every single grave has been emptied!"

He looked up at the grey sky as small needles of stinging snow fell silently from it. "Just what in hell's name was that light?" he asked.

The Royal Canadian Mounted Police searched with every available man and found nothing. They searched for years and never found a clue to the mysterious disappearance of twelve hundred people. People who believe in alien unidentified flying objects (UFOs) think there is a link with the lights seen in the sky at the same time. No one else has been able to come up with a more sensible explanation.

Unidentified Flying Fears – FACT FILE

1. Unidentified flying objects (UFOs) have been blamed for many mysterious disappearances including . . .
– ships and aircraft that have vanished in the so-called Bermuda Triangle
– Missing satellites that have been lost while orbiting the earth.

2. UFOs have also been used to explain mysterious appearances such as . . .
– the Loch Ness Monster
– the Pyramids of Egypt – built by humans under the guidance of alien Pharaohs
– Jesus – who was a flying-saucer pilot from Saturn.

3. Ninety per cent of UFOs are explained as natural or human happenings. People have usually seen . . .the planet Venus, aircraft, comets, meteors, giant balloons, cloud formations, ball lightning, army or shipping flares, or even flocks of migrating geese.

4. UFO experts (Ufologists) have different ideas about where aliens might come from. They say they come from . . .
– Mars – the number of UFO sightings is very high when Mars is at its closest point to earth

– the Milky Way – though *we* know nothing which travels fast enough to reach us from there . . . perhaps aliens do
– the earth itself – aliens reached us years ago and live in colonies on earth (the South Pole being a popular idea)
– inside the earth – with the entrance over the North Pole.

5.   Ufologists cannot agree on what the aliens want with us. They say the aliens . . .
– see earth as a sort of entertaining "zoo" of strange human animals
– want to examine us to see what makes us work (and there are hundreds of stories where aliens are supposed to have kidnapped, examined and released victims)
– want to take over earth because their own planet is dying
– do *not* want to take over the earth, but want to keep an eye on us because they are worried about what humans will do if or when they finally develop space travel
– want to make friends and share their knowledge with us.

6.   Reports of strange sightings go back to the thirteenth century when monks at St Albans sighted "a ship, large, elegantly shaped and well-equipped and of a marvellous colour", while monks in Yorkshire saw "a

large round silver disc" flying over their heads. Glowing discs covered the sky of Switzerland in 1566, while a whole stream of saucers flew over Embrun in France in 1820.

7.   Strange marks began to appear in cornfields in Britain in the 1980s – huge circles and patterns that some people believed could only be made by alien visitors. Other people have shown how the circles could easily be faked, but the Ufologists refused to believe them! An even more weird theory is that the circles were made by hedgehogs trampling the corn! Then someone worked out it would take 40,000 hedgehogs charging round together to make even one small crop circle!

8.   It's believed that a flying saucer crashed in New Mexico, USA, in 1947. The army discovered it and described a "flying disc". But the next day they changed their story. They said it was simply a crashed weather balloon. Ufologists think the army is trying to hide the truth so that people won't be frightened. William Moore, an American, has been working since 1977 trying to prove that an alien craft really did crash and that the army is lying.

9.   There is a vast and unexplored area of the earth where thousands of alien spacecraft could hide . . . the oceans of the world. Two women say they were kidnapped by aliens and examined. The mushroom-shaped spaceships came out of the sea off the coast of Brazil. The aliens looked like huge rats with narrow slits for mouths; they had thin arms and grey, sticky skin. The aliens told the women that they had a base at the South Pole and a tunnel that took them out under the ice.

·A·
KILLING
in KILDARE

Ireland is a country famous for its links with the supernatural. In Ireland no evil-doer is safe from the sort of freak bad luck that befell the killer of County Kildare . . .

Kildare, Eire – 1880

The body should have stayed hidden forever. It was buried in a shallow grave beneath the fine green turf.

But this was Ireland.

Patrick Freeley and his son, Sean, left their cottage and crossed the fields and began to push their wooden spades into the turf. Just beneath the surface was the mush of brown and rotten plants – peat. It would dry out and make fine, slow-burning fuel to see them through the winter.

"Father!" Sean cried suddenly. "I broke my spade!"

The old man straightened and rubbed his aching back. "You always were a careless lad, Sean," he sighed.

"No, father. It hit something hard under the turf," the boy argued.

"Probably a log . . . I'll dig it out for you," Patrick offered.

He pushed the spade carefully into the peat and found the solid thing that blocked his way. The old man slid the spade under the thing. He gave a quick twist of his strong wrists and hauled it out of the ground.

"Holy Mother!" Sean croaked and crossed himself quickly.

His father stepped back and the thing fell back into its peat grave. A flabby, white human hand on the end of a long-dead arm. Patrick muttered a quick prayer then set about uncovering the rest of the body.

He removed the covering turf as gently as a nurse might remove a bandage. The clothes were stained dark with the long soaking in their damp, brown tomb – they looked curiously old-fashioned to young Sean, who was just sixteen.

The face appeared like a pale, sad moon. It was fresh as the day it had died. Patrick knelt on the damp earth and brushed away strands of peat from the young features. "Ah, Michael," he murmured. "Praise God, you're dead."

"You know him, Father?" Sean asked.

Patrick rose and his creased face was pinched with pain. "Aye. And his father, poor old Tom Deeley. I wish old Tom had lived long enough to see this."

"To see his son dead?" Sean gasped. "What father in his right mind would want to live to see his son dead?"

"Tom Deeley would," Patrick said. He took a piece of turf and folded it carefully over the face. A sign of respect before he stood and looked over the folds of the hills. "Let's leave this to the police, shall we?"

The two peat-cutters set off down the brown path between the green banks towards the nearest town. "Young Michael Deeley was a wild lad," Patrick began. "Full of fun and mischief . . . but no real wickedness. And he had a dream. A dream that he'd go to America and make his fortune. He was desperate to save enough money to go. But saving money was hard in those days. Times are hard now . . . they were harder then. So, when he disappeared, folk said he'd gone to America."

"But, Father, why did you say that it was good that he was dead?" Sean asked.

"Young Michael had offered to take two bullocks to market for me. He'd done it before and I trusted him. He'd sell them at market and bring me the money. It saved me a journey and I'd give him a little towards his American dream. But that last time he never came back. I went to Tom Deeley's house to see if he'd come home. He hadn't. We waited up till midnight. We thought maybe he'd stopped at the market for a drink or two . . ."

"But he never came home?" Sean said.

"No. Of course old Tom was upset enough at Michael's disappearance. We thought maybe he'd been robbed on the way home. But what really hurt Tom Deeley was when folk started putting around a story that young Michael had gone to America," Patrick explained.

Sean nodded. "He could have sold your bullocks, pocketed the money and gone on the next ship."

"Aye. I never believed it myself, but it hurt old Tom to know people were calling his son a thief," the man said. "And there was nothing he could do to prove otherwise. The shame took him to an early grave. As I said, he'd rather see his son dead than branded a thief. And the village never quite forgot young Michael Deeley. Just last week we were talking about him in the tavern."

"That's strange, father," the boy said.

"You see, it was just twenty-one years last month since Michael disappeared. Now, as you know, you can sign up for twenty-one years' service in an American city and retire on a grand pension. If Michael had gone to America then he'd have been due home about now with that fortune he dreamed of." The man sighed. "At least he can come home to the village churchyard and lie with his father and mother."

The peat-cutters fell silent and marched the seven miles to the nearest town.

Police Sergeant Shannon was not going to walk seven miles to look at a long-dead body. "We'll take the pony and cart!" he announced. So he set off with the Freeleys to the site of the lonely burial.

"Aye!" Sergeant Shannon shouted over the clatter of the wheels. "I wish old Tom had lived to see this!"

"Just what I was telling young Sean," Patrick Freeley agreed.

"Whoa!" the policeman cried and hauled on the reins of the patiently plodding pony. A stranger was standing by the side of the narrow road to let the cart pass. But Police Sergeant Shannon was the sort of man who liked to know everyone's business. "Good afternoon!" he called. "Would you be heading our way, sir, and could we offer you a lift?"

The stranger smiled. "Mighty kind of you," he grinned and climbed onto the cart.

"American, are you?" the curious sergeant asked.

"No, I just spent twenty-one years there and I guess I picked up the accent," the man said. "I'm a native of County Kildare."

Sergeant Shannon noticed the man's fine cloth suit and embroidered waistcoat. "You must have had a good job in America!"

The stranger stuck out his heavy jaw and said proudly, "Twenty-one years with the Boston police force. Rose to the rank of lieutenant."

"It's a policeman you are, is it!" Sergeant Shannon said, delighted. For the rest of the journey he told the stranger of his own great deeds in the Kildare police service.

It was an hour later when Patrick Freeley called, "Stop here, Sergeant Shannon!" and the policeman pulled the cart to a halt.

"Why are we stopping?" the stranger asked.

"Ah, it's a case you might be interested in yourself!" he cried. "You being a famous Boston policeman may be able to help me solve the mystery of the man in the peat!"

"What man?"

"Come along and see," the sergeant urged.

Slowly, reluctantly, the stranger followed the three men to the shallow grave beneath the turf. He stayed silent while the Irish policeman peeled back the turf that covered the face of Michael Deeley. Sergeant Shannon placed a hand beneath the dead man's head to lift it clear of the grave. "The skull's been crushed at the back here! I think that makes it murder, don't you?" he asked.

The stranger had turned as pale as the dead man. "It should be a skeleton," he whispered in horror. "It should be rotted beyond recognition years ago!" His jaw hung loosely open and his eyes reflected the purple hills like pools of solid glass.

The sergeant nodded, " 'Tis the minerals in the peat, they say. Preserves a body like one of those mummies. But this is the body of Michael Deeley all right!"

Then something strange and horrifying happened. As the sergeant lifted the head further forward, the body folded at the waist and a jet of water gushed from the mouth.

The water stained the fine brown boots of the stranger and he gave a choking cry, "No, Michael! Michael, forgive me!"

Sergeant Shannon asked, "You know this man, then?"

The stranger's eyes were fixed on the corpse and he spoke quickly, his Irish accent returning stronger than ever. "He looks just the way he did the day I killed him. He was so proud of the money he'd made at the market. Ten pounds for those two bullocks. Ten pounds. And all I needed for my passage to America was those ten pounds. And I followed him. Followed him as he made his way back home in the dark. I hit him with a branch – I didn't mean to kill him!"

"But you did," Sergeant Shannon said and his voice was cold as Michael Deeley's grave.

"But I did. I buried him here . . . I went to America. I wrote home from time to time. They never said they found the body! I thought I was safe! Safe!"

"You'll hang for this murder," Sergeant Shannon said.

The stranger nodded. "Michael's just been waiting for this moment, haven't you, Michael?" the stranger whispered.

"Michael could wait," Patrick Feeley said bitterly. "The shame is his poor old father, Tom, couldn't."

Sergeant Shannon took the stranger roughly by the arm. "You're right, Patrick. I wish old Tom Freeley had lived long enough to see this!"

The stranger was too shaken to ever deny the murder. "Justice" had waited twenty-one years to catch him. He pleaded guilty and died on the end of a hangman's rope.

Irish Horror – FACT FILE

1. Irish legends are famous for their "fairy people" – but their "fairies" aren't cute little ladies with wings and magic wands. They're almost human in size, sometimes taller, and not always kindly towards humans. They can lure you to their country with their haunting music and make you their slave.

2. One Irish story tells of a man whose wife was kidnapped by the fairy people. He could only rescue her by throwing a jug of fresh milk over her as she rode past on Hallowe'en. Unfortunately the milk had two drops of water in it so the spell didn't work. His wife fell from her horse, the fairy people gathered round her. She disappeared . . . but left a ghastly trail of blood on the road. This was the revenge of the fairy people.

3.   Irish graveyards can also be dangerous. A young man went to the funeral of his girlfriend. As he stood alone by her grave a young woman came and spoke to him. She made him promise to meet her there in three weeks' time. She then asked him to seal the agreement with a kiss. As he gave her the kiss her head turned into a skull. This hideous vision drove him mad. Within three weeks he was dead. He was carried to his grave . . . and he carried out his promise to meet the young woman again in the graveyard.

4.   The Irish word for "fairy woman" is "banshee", but banshee has come to mean something else. It is the phantom that haunts the members of one particular family. When someone in the family is about to die, the banshee appears and gives a horrible wail. A death is sure to follow.

5.   A belief in fairy people has led to at least one horrific death in Ireland. Michael Cleary believed that his wife had been kidnapped by the fairies. The woman he was living with was, he thought, not his wife but a fairy who had been sent to take her place. He tortured his poor wife by roasting her over an open fire. He had the help of eight members of her family. Michael Cleary swore that it could not have been his wife they

killed . . . the dead woman was two inches taller than his wife so she had to be a witch-fairy. He was sentenced to twenty years' hard labour while the others went to prison. Irish children still sing the street song:

> *"Are you a witch? Are you a fairy?*
> *Or are you the wife of Michael Cleary?"*

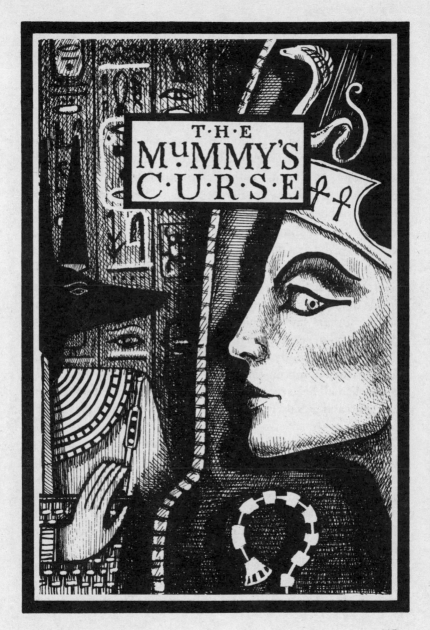

THE
MUMMY'S
CURSE

Some of the greatest events in history seem cursed before they have even begun. And sometimes that curse has been waiting 3,000 years to happen!

Egypt – 1890

The mummy of Princess Amen-Ra should have been left to rest in peace. She was evil enough in life . . . she was worse after death. She gave the orders that led to more than a hundred men being sold as slaves or cruelly executed. Then Princess Amen-Ra was stabbed by one of her lovers. She died fifteen hundred years before the birth of Christ. As was the custom, her body was preserved as a mummy.

It was dried in salts and wrapped in bandages. And magical charms and spells were written on reed-paper and wrapped inside the bandages. Some say the charms were to scare off evil spirits. Others say the charms were a curse that would bring doom to whoever disturbed the princess's rest.

Her charmed body was placed in a stone coffin and hidden in a deep rock-tomb on the banks of the Nile. The Pyramids' tombs had all been robbed. The rock-tombs seemed safer from the grim and greedy grave-robbers. But eventually they found her.

They robbed her tomb of all the gold and treasures that lay beside her. Then the robbers were left with just her mummy in its coffin. Worthless to the thieves . . . unless they could find someone willing to buy the three-thousand-year-old lady. They were in luck. Mummies had become fashionable in Victorian Britain. People bought mummified hands and feet as decorations for their homes!

Now four young men arrived at Luxor, keen to take souvenirs home. The thieves must have rubbed their hands in greedy glee. The four young men drew lots. The winner got to buy and keep the mummy in her fine stone coffin.

The winner paid the thieves in cash; it cost him several hundred pounds. He had the coffin taken to the hotel where he was staying. That was when the curse began to waken from its ancient sleep and work upon the men. The first young man, the one who bought the mummy, said, "I'm going for a walk!"

He walked towards the desert. He was never seen again.

Next day the second man began to argue with his Egyptian servant. The servant drew a gun and shot the young man in the arm. The wound began to fester. The surgeon only saved the young man's life by cutting off his arm.

The third young man went home to dreadful news. His whole life's savings were in a bank . . . the bank had failed and all his money had been lost.

The fourth young man fell ill, too ill to work. He lost his job and ended his days selling matches on the streets.

The stone coffin, or sarcophagus, came to England where a businessman in London bought old Amen-Ra.

He gave it to the British Museum – it seems that three of his family were injured in an accident, then his house caught fire not long after the mummy reached his home.

The museum took the gift. The cart arrived in the museum yard. As it was being unloaded the horse took fright and pushed backwards. The cart skidded over the cobbles and crashed into a wall. It trapped a passer-by. He ended up in hospital.

Two workmen carried Amen-Ra into the building. As they climbed the stairs the coffin slipped. The first man fell and broke his leg. The second went home quite healthy . . . then died just two days later.

Surely Princess Amen-Ra should now rest in peace? She couldn't. Watchmen heard her crying in her coffin. Priceless things inside her room were lifted up and dropped. One museum keeper claimed that he had been attacked.

Cleaners would not, of course, go near the withered lady. One man flicked her with a duster just to show that he was not afraid. Within the week his child had died of measles.

So Amen-Ra was locked away and her case was taken to the basement where she'd do no harm.

A newspaper took the story and sent their best photographer. But something happened to the photo – when it was developed it showed a face so fierce and hideous that it scared him half to death. They say he shot himself that night.

The museum sold the mummy and her coffin to another collector. But when a guest said that she'd seen the mummy rise and walk towards her then he had to sell it.

No museum wanted Amen-Ra. No collector had the nerve to take the risk. At last a fearless archaeologist from the United States said he would buy the cursed coffin and the evil Princess Amen-Ra.

It was loaded onto the huge ocean liner and placed in a special compartment behind the bridge on which the captain stood. It was too valuable to be lowered deep into the hold at the bottom of the ship with all the other rich treasures.

She seemed to lie there quietly enough, but . . .

April 1912 – The Atlantic Ocean

On the top deck of the liner the last passengers yawned and stretched and thought about going to their cabins for the night. Mrs Ida Straus turned to her husband. "One more walk along the deck, Isidor, before we go down to our cabin?" she suggested.

He looked over his gold-rimmed glasses. "It's very cold out there," he said.

"But very beautiful," she urged. "Come along. The fresh air will do you good!"

He sighed. It was never any use arguing with Ida when she'd made her mind up about something. He helped his wife into her coat and they stepped onto the deck.

The sea was darker than Isidor's rich black boots, and perfectly calm. The sky was moonless but blazing with bright stars. The liner trembled slightly as the powerful motors pushed it across the Atlantic and the only sound was the band playing somewhere below in the ballroom.

At first Ida thought the deck was deserted. Then she saw the glow of a cigar. A man was standing at the far rail. "Good evening! Lovely evening!" Mrs Straus called.

The man turned and nodded. He held out a hand to Isidor. "Good evening, sir. I'm William Stead."

"Ah, the writer!" Isidor said, shaking the hand of the man with the thick grey beard. "This is my wife, Ida, and I am Isidor Straus."

"Mmm, the congressman and banker," Stead nodded.

"I like your stories, Mr Stead. Good adventures. A good read!" Isidor said eagerly.

"Ooh!" his wife shivered. "Too gruesome for me!"

Stead looked surprised. "Gruesome, Mrs Straus? Which of my stories could you consider gruesome?"

"The ones about talking to spirits of the dead," she said firmly.

"You don't believe in such things?" the writer asked.

"I do. That's why they scare me!" she smiled but didn't look too scared. "Is that what you're doing out here? Talking to the spirits of the Atlantic?"

Stead laughed. "No . . ."

"Spirits of this ship, then? Surely it's too new to have ghosts of old dead sailors on board!" Ida chuckled. The banker sensed that there was something Stead was holding back. "But?"

"It's nothing."

"Come on, man! What do you know about this ship that's so secret?" Isidor urged.

Stead shrugged. "A feeling. Something uncomfortable. Something I sense every time I go near the bridge of the ship."

"No need to worry, Mr Stead," Ida said and patted his arm. "Someone told me yesterday that God himself couldn't sink this ship."

"Stead won't believe that, my dear!" Isidor laughed. "I seem to remember he once wrote a story about a disaster at sea. An unsinkable ship that sank! Isn't that right, Mr Stead?"

"That was twenty years ago," he said.

"Don't worry," Isidor said to his wife. "If the spirits had told him that this ship would sink then he wouldn't be here now, would you, Mr Stead?"

The banker blinked. "Mr Stead? Mr Stead!"

"Oh . . . sorry, Mr Straus . . ." the writer stammered.

"What are you looking at?" Isidor demanded.

"A patch on the stars – look to the right. The stars are filling the sky . . . but over there . . . follow my arm . . . see! Something huge blotting them out!"

"Good lord!" Ida exclaimed. "What on earth can it be?"

Stead licked his lips which were strangely dry. "It's monstrous! Some sort of shadow across the stars! It's getting bigger every second!"

"No!" Isidor said firmly. "It's just that we're getting closer."

Suddenly a faint voice cut the crystal air. "Iceberg dead ahead!"

"Ahh!" Ida Straus sighed. "Just an iceberg! You were beginning to frighten me there, Mr Stead, with your stories of sinking ships and shadows swallowing the ship."

Stead gave a weak smile. "Sorry, Mrs Straus. Yes, we can see it now. Now that the lights of the ship are catching it. Just a huge block of ice!"

"Huge indeed!" Isidor gasped. "Why, it's higher than the mast . . . and so far south, who'd believe it?"

"Ah, the ship's turning now. We're going to miss it," Ida murmured.

As she spoke, the ship swung slightly and brushed against the mountain of ice. The deck beneath their feet shuddered as it scraped against the much larger mountain below the waterline. The iceberg passed out of sight behind them.

"So, your horrors of something fearful lurking on this ship were wrong, Mr Stead. Come inside and we'll have one last drink. I think the bars are still open," Ida smiled and led the way into the warm saloon.

Stead followed slowly. He still felt uneasy. The ship had drifted to a halt. Somewhere below there was the sound of clattering feet and anxious voices.

Ida Straus took his arm gently. "You worry too much, Mr Stead. Everyone knows the *Titanic* cannot sink!"

Five *Titanic* Truths – FACT FILE

1. Isidor Straus and his wife died when the *Titanic* sank. Women and children were offered the places in the lifeboats first – she refused to go without her husband, saying, "We started together and, if need be, we'll finish together." They made sure that their maid was safe then went, arm in arm, back to their cabin to wait to die. Like many others that April night, they died so that others would have the chance to live.

2. William Stead wrote his story of the liner disaster in 1892. It was remarkably like the real disaster of the *Titanic* twenty years later – but it didn't stop him making the trip. He was last seen reading alone in one of the smoking rooms. A crewman, passing the room, said he looked as if he planned to stay there whatever happened. Stead was never seen again.

3.   Stead's story was an amazing prediction. But a writer called Morgan Robertson came up with an even stranger tale. His story, *Futility*, told of a liner that was the largest and finest ever built – just like the *Titanic*.

– On its maiden voyage across the Atlantic it hit an iceberg and sank – just like the *Titanic*.

– It lost more passengers than it need have because it carried too few lifeboats – just like the *Titanic*.

– Robertson's ship was 800 feet long; the *Titanic* was 882.

– Robertson's ship had three propellers; so had the *Titanic*.

– Robertson's ship hit the iceberg at 25 knots; the *Titanic*, 23.

– Robertson's ship had twenty-four lifeboats; *Titanic*, twenty.

– Robertson's ship sank in April; so did the *Titanic*.

Robertson wrote his story in 1898, ten years before the *Titanic* was even dreamed of. So the most amazing "true" fact of all is the name he gave to his ship – the *Titan*!

4.   The sinking of the *Titanic* is a particularly famous sea disaster because so many famous people died that night, about fifteen hundred of the two thousand and three hundred people on board lost their lives, and because she was supposed to be unsinkable. But it is nowhere near the "worst" sea disaster for loss of

innocent lives. That was on 30 January 1945 when a Russian submarine sank a German passenger ship and killed about 7,700 of the 8,700 men, women and children on board.

5.   The story of Amen-Ra's mummy and the curse is a popular legend – but it is much harder to find any serious proof that the curse was at work or that the coffin was even on the *Titanic*. People who tell the mummy story say she was put on the ship secretly so the passengers wouldn't be worried. This is why there is no proper record of it being there.

True Monster Stories
by *Terry Deary*

Incredible? Impossible? Too awful to imagine? But someone, somewhere at some time has sworn that each of these strange stories is true . . .

Read accounts of the Yeti, the vampire, and less well-known beasts, like Black Dog and Mogawr; consider the facts and decide for yourself whether these monster stories really are true. And even if you choose not to believe, beware! These tales may linger in your thoughts and darken your dreams . . .

HORRIBLE HISTORIES
History with the nasty bits left in!

The Awesome Egyptians
by *Terry Deary* and *Peter Hepplewhite*

The Awesome Egyptians gives you some awful information about phabulous Pharaohs and poverty-stricken peasants – who lived an awesome 5,000 years ago!

> Want to Know:
> ★ which king had the worst blackheads?
> ★ why some kings had to wear false beards?
> ★ why the peasants were revolting?

In this book you'll find some foul facts about death and decay, revolting recipes for 3,000-year-old sweets, how to make a mean mummy, and some awful Egyptian arithmetic.

History has *never* been so horrible!

The Terrible Tudors
by *Terry Deary* and *Neil Tonge*

The Terrible Tudors gives you all the grizzly details of Tudor life for everyone – from cruel kings and queens, to poor peasants and common criminals.

> Want to Know:
> ★ some terrible Tudor swear words?
> ★ about terrible Tudor torture?
> ★ why Henry VIII thought he'd married a horse?

Read this book to find some foul facts, some horrendous beheadings, a mysterious murder, some curious quizzes and gruesome games.

History has *never* been so horrible!

HIPPO HUMOUR

COPING WITH ...

Coping With School
by *Peter Corey* illustrated by *Martin Brown*

Peter Corey is back at school, looking into locker rooms, delving into school dinners and peering into playgrounds. Don't think you can survive the happiest days of your life without this essential guide.

Coping With Parents
by *Peter Corey* illustrated by *Martin Brown*

A must for all parent owners!

Do you have one or more parents? And do you find them a problem? Don't worry – you're not alone in your troubles. In fact, 99% of people questioned admitted that their parents are an aggravation to them!
This book is *your* chance to hit back! Learn what makes parents tick, how to reorganize different types of parents, and then begin a step-by-step programme to getting even!

Coping With Teachers
by *Peter Corey* illustrated by *Martin Brown*

Is everyone always telling you that school days are the best days of your life? Do you wonder how this can possibly be when there's always some teacher lurking around just waiting to spoil all your fun?
In Coping with Teachers, Peter Corey (4b) turns intrepid investigator in an effort to understand what makes teachers tick. He visits the natural habitats of 26 species of teacher, revealing fascinating facts that will shock and amaze.

Coping With Boys/Coping With Girls
by *Peter Corey* and *Kara May*

An unusual interpretation of the battle of the sexes!
Peter Corey is back, and this time he's brought a friend. While Peter does battle with the girls, flip over the book and Kara May answers back about boys. From the dawn of history right through to the present day, these two-books-in-one provide an hilarious and illuminating two-sided and sometimes directly contradicting view of the battle of the sexes.

You Be The Jury
by *Marvin Miller*

Did Mr Rogers fake his burglary to claim the insurance money?
Is Stanley Woot's last will and testament a fake?
Did John Goode shoot his business partner by accident – or was it attempted murder?

Ten intriguing courtroom mysteries are played out before you. Examine each case, study the evidence, then make your decision. The final verdict is up to you!

You Be The Jury II
by *Marvin Miller*

Here we have twenty more intriguing courtroom mysteries for you to solve.

Which one of the identical Lee twins vandalised Farmer Foley's chicken coup?
Did Brenda Taylor deliberately set fire to her jewellery shop so she could claim the insurance money?

Examine each case, study the evidence, then make your decision. The final verdict is up to you!

You Be The Jury III
by *Marvin Miller* illustrated by *Harry Venning*

Order in the Court!

The court is now in session and *you* are the jury!
In these ten mysterious cases *you* must examine the evidence, *you* spot the clues, and *you* decide the verdict – Guilty or not guilty.

You Be The Detective
by *Marvin Miller*

Can YOU solve the crime?

Seven baffling crimes have been committed, and YOU are the detective. You have to visit the scene of the crime, question the suspects and piece together the clues.

Who Dunnit?
by *Marvin Miller* illustrated by *Harry Venning*

A brilliant book for all budding detectives, with picture puzzle crimes to solve, a complex collection of codes to crack, hints on how to search for clues – in fact, everything you need to become a supersleuth.